Kate Pullinger was born in British Columbia and came to the UK in her twenties. Her previous books include the novels *Weird Sister*, *The Last Time I Saw Jane*, and *Where Does Kissing End?* (the latter published by Serpent's Tail), and the short story collections *My Life as a Girl in a Men's Prison* and *Tiny Lies*. She also writes for film, radio and the digital media; you can find her latest multi-media piece at www.katepullinger.com.

She has been writer-in-residence at HMP Gartree, Fellow in Creative Writing at the University of Reading, the Judith E Wilson Visiting Fellow at Jesus College, Cambridge, Visiting Writing Fellow at The Women's Library, London Metropolitan University, and the Royal Literary Fund's Virtual Fellow. She currently teaches on the MA in Creative Writing at UEA, and the MA in Creative Writing and Technology at De Montfort University.

Kate Pullinger lives in London with her family.

Praise for *A Little Stranger*

'Beautifully written and executed' ***Daily Mail***

'Pullinger brilliantly depicts the murky and often dull challenge of looking after a toddler, unleavened by adult company. But underlying this is the universal fear that we will become the Bad Mother, replicating our worst traits in our children in an unending cycle... This is a witty, charming and highly readable novel, laced with an exploration of those primal fears that stubbornly remain taboo among mothers' ***Independent***

'Brilliantly conveyed... a must read' ***Grazia***

'Her ear for what is not said is pitch perfect, as is her sense of the mess people make of themselves and each other' ***TLS***

'Gripping, sharp and brilliantly kind. She knows the gamble that life is and she never once flinches. Her books are always revelations. What a good read' **Ali Smith**

'Kate Pullinger's acutely perceptive writing, compassionate and haunted, excels at conveying the grey areas between life's certainties... It retains the gripping quality of a thriller' *Metro London*

'Interspersed with poignant flashbacks about families and relationships, *A Little Stranger* is a beautifully crafted novel with a bloody beating heart' *Diva*

'A gripping exposé of the problems of nuclear families in this day and age... Pullinger is deft with language and resists cliché for her characters, giving us a quietly uplifting book with real heart' *The List*

'A beautifully written, well-crafted, page-turning novel' *Glasgow Evening Times*

'*A Little Stranger* dares to be shockingly honest... A little stranger is a startling exploration of the effects of familial relationships' *Big Issue*

'This is a poignant tale exploring how we all, as individuals, fit within and connect with our respective families. Kate Pullinger beautifully evokes a sense of bittersweet contemporary family life. An absorbing read' *Buzz*

A LITTLE STRANGER

KATE PULLINGER

A complete catalogue record for this book can
be obtained from the British Library on request

The right of Kate Pullinger to be identified as the author of this work has
been asserted by her in accordance with the Copyright, Designs and Patents
Act 1988

First published in Canada in 2004 by McArthur & Company, Toronto

First published in the UK in 2006 by Serpent's Tail

First published in this 5-star edition in 2007 by Serpent's Tail
an imprint of Profile Books Ltd
3A, Exmouth House
Pine Street
Exmouth Market
London EC1R 0JH
www.serpentstail.com

Printed in the UK by CPI Bookmarque, Croydon, CR0 4TD

10 9 8 7 6 5 4 3 2

'Disobedience' is taken from *When We Were Very Young* © A A Milne.
Published by Egmont UK Limited, London and used with permission

For my own mother
who is nothing like
Fran or Ireni

James James
Morrison Morrison
Weatherby George Dupree
Took great
Care of his Mother,
Though he was only three.
James James
Said to his Mother,
"Mother," he said, said he:
"You must never go down to the end of the town,
If you don't go down with me."

From *Disobedience* by A.A. Milne

ESCAPE

A woman stands on her own beside the baggage carousel. All around her there is noise: people talking, bored and tired after their long flights, the tannoy announcing delays, departures, arrivals, lost passengers, lost bags, the machinery of the long metal conveyer belt starting up and then shutting down again, the soft clunk and slide as yet another bag emerges, people wrestling with their baggage trolleys; if she listened hard enough she would hear, outside the terminal building, the sound of airplanes overhead, their great wings straining, tires meeting the tarmac with short sharp screeches, she would hear the motorized luggage carriers, she would hear the catering trucks, the fuel lorries, she would hear the flight controllers up in their tower talking about what they watched on TV last night. But she hears nothing. She stands alone, in blessed silence. She has no bags to collect, all she carries is her small, well-made leather handbag, but she stays beside the carousel locked into some kind of unthinking repeat behaviour pattern, a race memory of air travel, of all the air journeys she has made in her life. There is no one meeting her, there is no one speaking to her, no one tugging at her dress. She is in a silent room, a white room, a room devoid of clutter; there is a vase of flowers, sunshine, white linen bed sheets — everything clear, everything clean. It is a longed-for space, a dream room, a place where she can be by herself. She is there now. She is free.

The thing is, I'm just not up to it. I'm not capable. I thought I was, of course I did. Everyone does it. Well, most people do it, most women, at least. It's natural, some people say it's a fundamental right; how hard can it be? My own mother did it and did it well, at least initially, until I was eight or so, and those eight years set me up for life. All around me people do it, in conditions far worse than mine: single parents — there's a woman I see in the park who has four kids and she's on her own and they look happy, healthy. Refugees. People who are disabled; people whose kids are disabled; people who have cancer; people who have no jobs and no money and live on benefits in bad housing: they all do it and most of them do it pretty well.

And then there's me.

So I've resolved to do something about it. I'm not sure what, haven't got to that yet. I'm trying to think it through but my powers of independent thought aren't what they used to be. It's got to happen though; things must change. Before something awful happens. Before I can no longer remember how to be happy.

Fran was lying in bed, trying to read a novel.

She couldn't clear her head of what had happened earlier in the day. She'd taken Louis to the shops. They'd gone into the organic supermarket to buy bread. Fran thought she should buy organic — it was better for Louis, it was better for all of them. But they couldn't afford it. Everything cost twice as much as it did elsewhere. And the produce, flown in from the world over — tiny bright orange mangoes from Sri Lanka, dripping papaya from Gambia, fat runner beans from Madagascar — tended to go off if it wasn't eaten right away. This made her wonder about the fruit and vegetables she bought in the ordinary supermarket, lettuce that didn't wilt, tomatoes that lasted forever — were preservatives injected on the vine?

She was buying bread; it was expensive but, Fran thought, superior enough to justify the price. At the organic supermarket, as in any other supermarket, they kept the sweets — organic sweets — near the till. Louis spotted his favourite, strips of dried fruit that were like candied leather. For ages Fran had thought these were good treats to give to Louis, they were made of fruit after all, completely natural; then one day her dentist told her they were worse than chocolates and crisps because of their tendency to adhere to the teeth. So no more fruit strips for Louis. He got up out of his pushchair — the shop was full of stairs that she'd had to lug Louis, the pushchair, and the shopping up and down, in relays — and marched over to the shelf. He pointed, smiled, and said 'Please'. Fran was counting her coins. She had enough money for the bread, nothing else. She couldn't believe Louis had said please. She was tempted to put the bread back and buy him the sweet instead. But they needed the bread. She needed the bread. So, she said no, there wasn't enough money, and told him to get into the pushchair.

There was a brief lull. Fran paid for the bread and put it in her bag. She turned to face Louis.

He threw himself on the floor and started to wail.

Fran stood absolutely still. She couldn't move; Louis was nothing but movement. He kicked his arms and feet out, suddenly looking surprisingly large. Other customers stepped over him, around him, glancing at Fran, telegraphing disapproval, distaste. One woman actually made that tutting noise. Fran looked away. Louis' tantrums filled her with wonder — the impossible fury of it all. 'Louis?' she said. He screamed more loudly. 'Louis,' she tried whispering, maybe whispering would stun him into submission. He kicked harder, more wildly.

And then she herself was filled with fury, a fury that felt as sudden, and large, as Louis' — Why me? Why now? I can't stand another minute of this. She wrenched the empty pushchair away from where it was parked and walked out of the shop.

The door closed behind her. She could no longer hear Louis. She pushed the chair along the street, past the clothes shops and cafés, down to the newsagent. She parked the pushchair, applied the brake, went inside, and looked at the tidy stacks of newspapers. She looked at the magazines, all those magazines she used to read every month in Celine's, those magazines that used to help her decide who she was, what she looked like, who she might be. Well, she wasn't glossy anymore. She no longer shopped for clothes, she no longer worked with clothes, and she no longer met up with her girl-friends to talk about these things.

She left the shop and looked at the pushchair. She could leave it there. She was next to a bus stop, any minute now a bus would come along and she could get on it. She could get on the bus and sit down, and look out the window. She could stare out the win-dow in peace. She could be stuck in a traffic jam for hours and hours and it wouldn't matter, she wouldn't care, she'd have no one to be concerned with, apart from herself. She could have a nap, she could file her nails. She wouldn't have to think of Louis. She wouldn't have to cook his tea. She wouldn't have to figure out how to stop him from screaming. She'd be back in control, of her life, of her time. She stood at the bus stop and watched people coming and going from the newsagent, making their way past the pushchair without taking much notice of it.

If a bus comes now, I'll take it.

She looked at her watch without seeing the time.

If a bus comes now, I'll get on it.

The man from the newsagent, an Indian man, a man from whom she'd bought papers many times, for many years, but with whom she'd never exchanged more than a few words, came out of his shop. He lit a cigarette. He looked at her, smiled, and looked down at the empty pushchair. Then he looked up at the sky and said, 'A bit of sunshine. How lovely.' His voice broke through the heavy afternoon air.

'Yes,' said Fran. She took a deep breath. 'Sunshine.' She stepped away from the bus stop, took hold of the handles of the pushchair, released the brake, and pushed it away, back down the street, past the clothes shops and the furniture shops, the antique dealers, the art gallery and the cafés, and into the organic super-market.

Louis was sitting on the floor. He had stopped crying. He was eating a fruit strip; someone must have given him one. When she entered the shop, he looked up at her and smiled and said, 'Mummy.' She didn't speak, but knelt down and gathered him into her arms, hugging him tight, then released him and smoothed his hair off his face. He smelled so sweet. He climbed into the pushchair and settled down, ready to be wheeled away, like an Emperor, benevolent ruler of his domain.

Their flat was small. It was on the first floor of a large Victorian house that had been converted in the 1960s. Up one flight on the narrow staircase; two flats above, one below. It was a good flat. Great location, lots of light. They'd stripped the floorboards and knocked down walls and made the kitchen and sitting room into one largish room and modernized the bathroom (white tiles, a shower, opaque glass). They'd spent money carefully. There was one bedroom and a little dressing room off it that now belonged to Louis. It was a small flat, but they were fine in it. They could walk to work. At least Nick could walk to work. Fran was no longer working.

She put down the novel she was trying to read. Louis was asleep in his cot in the next room and he wouldn't, shouldn't, wake up. Nick was at work. She knew she wouldn't be able to go to sleep, it was too early, she was too wound up. I should be used to nights in by myself. I should have invited someone around for a drink. Where are my friends? What's happened to all my friends? I haven't seen anyone for ages. I haven't seen Celine for at least a month. Celine was Fran's old employer; glamorous, childless, and nearly fifty, she was a Frenchwoman from Aix-en-Provence who had lived in London for many years. She never hesitated to make plain her horror of Fran's new life. 'Can't you get out, darling?' she'd say in her peculiar accent, as though her French vowels were being throttled by her English. 'Can't you slip round to my place?'

'Not tonight, Celine. Another day.'

'Why don't you come back to work for me?' Celine had asked this question a hundred times. 'I need you. The shop needs you. It's not the same without you — you must be bored—'

'I can't. You know I can't. We can't afford it. We can't afford for me to work.'

'Find a childminder, not a nanny, nannies are for the rich, a childminder, they're cheap, aren't they? An au pair. A Polish student. There must—'

'Celine, you don't pay enough for me to be able to afford to work for you. It's as simple as that.'

'There are perks.' Now Celine was insulted.

'Louis can't eat clothes.'

'But it's driving you mad. It's driving me mad watching you go mad.'

Fran didn't reply. What could she say?

Celine thought Louis was adorable; she liked to look at him, although that was as far as she went. Buying him clothes was one of her hobbies; she'd supplied the lavender cashmere BabyGro that had generated so much discussion down at the baby clinic.

But Fran couldn't go out, because she had to stay in. She would telephone Celine instead.

She got out of bed and put on her dressing gown. It was black quilted silk satin, French from the 1920s, in the style of a kimono. Wrapped up in it, she was warm and sleek. She put on her felt slippers — the very slippers, she thought, that she'd seen featured in a newspaper supplement just last week, chosen by an up-and-coming architect as her favourite design item — and left the bedroom. On the way down the short corridor she banged her ankle against the folded pushchair that was lying on the floor. She swore.

Fran hated the pushchair. She hated the way it dominated her life. She hated the way it ruled out public transport — buses and tube trains were impossible to negotiate. She hated the way it got stuck in doorways, in narrow shop aisles, on rough and uneven pavements. She hated the way that when she entered her favourite café the waiters' smiles faded once they saw what was coming. She hated the way she looked with it — she had become *one of them*, one of those women, harried, hunched, unattractive. Invisible. Some women wield their pushchairs like heavy artillery, flattening anyone who gets in their way. Others bowl along, straight-backed, Mary-Poppins-proud, breezy. Fran alternated — bad days, good days. This was her life now, and there was no getting away from it; the pushchair was necessary. She was as attached to it as it was to her. Just like the child. Louis.

London hates small children, Fran thought, London hates mothers like me. What has happened to me? I never used to be so angry. Or have I always been this way, waiting to blossom, like an enormous evil-smelling bud that opens in the night?

The pushchair usually resided downstairs in the front entrance hall. There wasn't anywhere else to put it, and Fran felt it was okay to leave it folded up and flat on the floor; if she tried to lean it against the wall it left marks and, inevitably, fell over. The other people who lived in the building didn't like having the pushchair there. 'Why can't you keep it in your flat?' Charlie, the woman downstairs, had asked once again, when Fran came in from her trip to the organic supermarket.

'Well,' Fran said slowly, 'here's how it is. I come into the house,' she demonstrated, miming, 'I've got Louis. I've got the shopping. I take Louis out of the chair and carry him upstairs. I stick him somewhere — in his cot or in his highchair — so that he can't escape and throw himself back down the stairs.'

Charlie smiled at that, Fran thought, malevolently.

'I come back down. I fold up the pushchair. I get the shopping. I carry that upstairs. By then, Louis is shouting. He doesn't want to be confined to his cot, or his high chair.'

'Oh yes,' said Charlie, 'I've heard him.'

'I take Louis out and calm him down. I unpack the shopping, which by then is melting, or spilling, or cracking, or whatever. Oh! Louis needs his nappy changing. Oh! Louis needs a bottle. Oh! I need a cup of tea. Or whatever.' Fran watched Charlie's face. 'By now, I'm too tired to go get the pushchair. I've forgotten about the pushchair. I don't fucking care about the pushchair.'

Charlie frowned.

'Could you bring it up to the flat for me?' Fran asked. 'That would be ever so helpful.'

Charlie grimaced as though in sympathy, and closed the door of her flat. Fran took a deep breath and turned to go up the stairs, Louis balanced on her hip.

The door opened once again. It was Charlie, wearing her art dealer smile, 'You did choose to have this baby, didn't you?'

Fran climbed the stairs without answering.

But later, when Louis was having his nap, she went downstairs and fetched the pushchair.

And now, she picked up the phone and went over to the settee. She and Nick had bought their sofa — dark red velvet upholstery, enormous soft cushions; a sofa big enough to live in, she liked to think — when Fran was still working. The furniture place down the road gave them a substantial discount; most of the local shop-keepers — the independents, not the more recent chains and franchises — helped each other out. Nick and Fran had bought most of what they owned that way. Fran dialed Celine's number and ran her hand along the back of the settee. Now the velvet was splattered with rough patches where Fran had scrubbed away Louis' sick.

'Hello?'

'It's me.'

'You! Hello. Where are you?'

'Where do you think?'

'Come over. Ruth and Jim are here. We're having champagne.'

'I can't.'

'Ooh,' said Celine, annoyed. 'Where's that Nick?'

'Where do you think?'

Fran looked at her watch. She was in her dressing gown and her slippers. It was midsummer, evening. Outside, the sun was still shining weakly.

'If he comes home early, my darling, come around and have a drink. We'll be at it 'til late.'

'Okay,' Fran said. She put the phone down and found herself close to tears.

She walked back into the bedroom. She sat down on the bed. She took a tissue and wiped her eyes. There was nothing to cry about. There was no point in crying. Charlie downstairs was right. They had chosen to have a baby. She had been out nearly every night between the ages of sixteen and thirty, she'd had enough nights out to last several lifetimes. Louis was more than a year and a half, he'd be two in the autumn, things were getting easier. He was a good sleeper. He had a good appetite. He had a reliable routine, regular naps, happy bathtimes. He was interested in books, toys, other children. He was a cheery soul, easy to take care of, apart from the tantrums. They'd been happening for about three months now. Fran couldn't decide if they were getting better, or worse. But it was not something to worry about, she knew, it was just a phase, one of many. She needed to learn a few more anti-tantrum tricks, that was all, and, more importantly, she needed to remember to use them.

Motherhood, for Fran, was surrounded by darkness. In the early days the darkness arose from lack of sleep; later it was deepened by loneliness. It was as though a bright hard white light shone down on her little family, Fran, Nick, and Louis, but outside of that ring of light — nothing. She tried peering into the dark when she was having a hard time, when she was tired, and when she needed help. She even tried calling out into it sometimes. 'Hello? Anybody out there?' But there was never any reply.

I would not have guessed that being a mother could be so boring. If I'd been asked what I thought it would be like (and I wasn't, of course, why would anyone ask me that?) I would not have said 'Boring'. But everyone who has done it knows there is a special tedium in caring for a small child, in the endless repetition of small yet vital tasks: feeding, changing, dressing, face-wiping, bathing, comforting, waking, sleeping. The absolute dependency that can feel both mind-numbingly inevitable and compellingly absorbing. And all of it completely inescapable.

Of course I love Louis, there is no question about that. I carried him inside my body for months, I gave birth to him, and he is a thing of beauty, with his flawless baby skin, his soft hair, his warm sticking-out tummy, his clean milky breath, his giggle. Every day he makes me laugh, every day seeing his face fills me with pleasure, every day he grows and changes. And he loves me as well, there's no doubt about that, with an awesome and consuming ferocity. There used to be a cartoon in the newspaper about an ordinary couple who'd given birth to an enormous baby, a baby as big as their sitting room. I didn't much like it at the time, but now I recall it and find myself thinking, yes, he is tiny but he occupies every corner of my life. How can something so small be so gargantuan?

And I am a rubbish mother. I know I am a rubbish mother. I know because I— ; I just know. Every day brings with it some new kind of failure: a tantrum that I failed to deal with properly, a demand — for sweets, perhaps — given into, an argument with Nick, brought on by fatigue. How hard can it be, taking care of a child? But I've discovered that nothing is simple. Nothing is easy.

I didn't have a temper before I had Louis. I can count the number of times I yelled at people before I had a baby; I used to shout at my mother when I was a teenager, and I shouted at my sister Sarah when we were kids. But apart from that, no one. Now I shout all the time. I shout at Louis when he has his tantrums, when he cries and shouts at me; 'Stop shouting!' I shout, 'Stop shouting!' I shout at Nick, well, pretty much all the time. I'm a rubbish mother, and I'm a lousy wife. It is awful, it is truly appalling, to do something so badly while being bored by it at the same time. And yet, that's my life. That's it. That's me.

Fran had tried, from time to time, to discuss it — what? this unnamed, unspoken, unspeakable, overwhelming feeling of failure, of failing every day, over and over again — with Nick. He couldn't do it. It wasn't that he didn't understand what she was saying, but, he said, there were some things that should simply not be discussed. There were some things that you were not allowed to say. End of conversation. Fran was shocked by his reticence; there had never been anything they couldn't talk about before. I need to talk about it, she wanted to say, maybe if I talk about it, it will go away. But they didn't. And it didn't. Instead they mostly talked about when — if — she would go back to work.

Fran remembered a conversation they had, not long after Louis was born. She was sitting on the red velvet settee. She had spent nearly an hour feeding the baby, propped up with a pillow behind her back, two pillows supporting Louis. He had finally fallen asleep — he had been awake and fretful all day, since early morning, not sleeping for more than ten minutes at a stretch. She put him into his moses basket on the floor next to the settee, tucked him up with a clean white blanket. His sweet elfin sleeping face. Nick brought Fran a cup of tea. He was making her something to eat — he had to go back out to work in half an hour. He flopped down beside her and gave her a hug. Her left nipple was cracked and bleeding, her stitches hurt, her back was still haunted by an epidural ache. She was at least two stone —

nearly thirty pounds — overweight. She sighed heavily, and let her husband hold her.

The baby woke up and began to scream, as though someone had come into the room and shaken him.

Fran burst into tears.

Nick picked up Louis — still scrawny and floppy, wrinkled and spotty, like a bag of frozen peas that had decided to fight for life — put him on his shoulder and tried to comfort him. It didn't work. Louis roared. He wanted Fran, he wanted her milk. But she couldn't bear the thought of feeding him yet again. When she was pregnant a friend had told her to massage her nipples with lanolin cream, in order to get ready for breastfeeding. 'Toughens them up,' she said. It didn't work. Fran's advice for pregnant women, advice that she would have willingly doled out had she been asked, was this: Try sandpaper, for a more realistic preparation.

Nick looked at Fran; she hadn't drunk her tea, she hadn't had a bath, she hadn't eaten her supper. But he didn't know what else he could do, apart from hand her the baby. How could a baby — a tiny, wee baby — render them both so incompetent?

Their problem, Nick thought, was they had no one to call. There was no one to lend a hand. Nick's parents were dead — his mum of breast cancer five years ago, his father of lung cancer two years before that. Nick's brother Robert was something in the City — a stockbroker or an insurance broker, Nick wasn't certain which. Being brothers didn't mean they had anything in common, and they spoke rarely, Christmas, birthdays. Nick's grandparents had been very present when Nick was a child; they lived in a flat around the corner and Nick's grandmother had taken care of Nick and Robert when their mother went out to work. But his grandparents were long dead as well. Fran's parents and only sibling were in Canada, thousands of miles away. There were no cousins nor aunts nor uncles. They had plenty of friends but they were either childless and uncomprehending or too busy with their own families. We are a nuclear family in the truest sense, Nick thought; a nuclear family about to go nuclear. Atomized.

Fran was still weeping. Not voluably, her shoulders weren't shaking — she was too tired for that. Just tears, running down her face.

And that's when she said it. She opened her mouth and out it came.

'We've made a mistake.'

Nick looked at his wife sharply. She saw that his face was grey with fatigue but he had on his dark green suit and he'd managed to iron a shirt and polish his shoes. He looked good, apart from his skintone and the bags under his eyes. He gave Louis — who had stopped howling but continued to shudder with huge after-sobs — a pat on the back.

'We've made a mistake.'

'You're not allowed to say that.'

But she had said it, and for that moment it was what she believed. They weren't cut out for parenthood. It was too much to expect. The baby took too much away from them, from Fran, from Nick. Not the baby, not Louis himself, but his existence. The very fact of his being alive. She didn't know what to do with him, how to stop him from crying. She wanted to send him back to where he came from, wherever that might be. She wanted her old life returned to her, intact.

Fran got up off the bed and opened the door of the closet. She found that when she didn't have to be somewhere, when she didn't have to meet anyone, it could be difficult to care about how she looked. She'd spent the months after Louis' birth in her pajamas. And then the pregnancy weight had finally come off and her clothes fit her once again; for the last few months she had resolved to try to dress properly. She hadn't bought anything new for a long time, but her old clothes still gave her pleasure.

She decided to get dressed. She'd get dressed and wait up for Nick, they could have a glass of wine when he came in. She put on a pair of slinky black trousers and a close-fitting top, a pair of high heels. She went over to where she kept her jewelry on top of the chest of drawers; earrings, a necklace, a couple of bracelets. Perfume. She went into the bathroom and made up her face. As with her clothes, she hadn't bought any new make-up for ages, but she'd collected so much over the years that it didn't matter, she still had plenty of slap for her face. She did her eyebrows, her lips; she covered up the dark half-moons under her eyes and put some blusher on her cheeks. She loved the fine powder, the way it clung to the brush and dusted her skin, translucent, vaguely shimmery. There, she was done. Finished. She smiled at her reflection. She looked okay.

She opened the fridge and took out a bottle of wine, popped the cork, and poured herself a glass. She left an empty glass on the counter, for when Nick returned. She went back to the sofa, and sat. And waited.

Ruth and Jim were at Celine's. Fran hadn't seen Ruth and Jim for ages. They were a good pair; he worked behind the scenes at the Royal Opera House, she was a freelance costume designer. Jim was very camp, loud and clever and bitchy; people who didn't know him always assumed he was gay. Ruth was more serious, quite shy. They'd been married for years and years, and did not have children. Celine and Fran had often speculated about whether or not Jim had boyfriends on the side; there was no evidence of this but they speculated anyway.

Celine and Ruth and Jim will be having an hilarious time, Fran thought. Jim guaranteed hilarity. Celine would be pouring champagne, and she'd be smoking one of her tightly rolled little joints. There'd be no food; Celine, skinny as a clothesrail, was always watching her weight, and she liked her friends to starve alongside her. They'd be playing Curtis Mayfield records; Curtis Mayfield provided the soundtrack for Celine's life. They'd be gossiping.

Fran went into Louis' room. He was sleeping soundly. He'd kicked off his blanket. It was a warm evening, but Fran adjusted his blanket anyway. They didn't have a baby monitor, the flat was so small they didn't need one. Fran wished that they had one. I could take it with me. She put on her jacket and picked up her handbag, checking for keys, money. She opened the door of the flat, stepped through, and closed it behind her. He's asleep. He'll stay asleep. And when he's asleep, he doesn't need me.

There were plenty of people out on the street. It was one of those summer evenings when Londoners pretend, with great conviction, to be European. The pavement was crowded with café tables, and drinkers from the pub spilled out as well. The air had a light, painterly quality to it. Celine lived above her shop a few streets away, ten minutes' walk. Fran strolled along, swinging her bag — oh god it felt good, to be out, to be free. She'd have a drink, she'd have a really big drink and a chat with her friends, and she'd have a drag off Celine's little joint. She wouldn't worry about when she had to be back, she wouldn't look at her watch. She wouldn't think about Louis. She'd be charming and funny and sophisticated and cosmopolitan and. . .

Then she saw it. Of course. Twenty-One. It was on the way to Celine's. Even Twenty-One had tables out on the street this evening. There was a queue of people standing next to the door. It wasn't the kind of place that encouraged queuing, it was too upmarket for that. But on such a warm, lovely evening people didn't mind queuing, they wanted to stand on the pavement with a drink, watching the world go by, laughing and talking, everyone at their best, on absolutely top form. Sometimes, Fran thought, London is full of beautiful people.

Fran watched the restaurant from the other side of the street. Nick came out the door, weighed down with plates. He was having to wait tables; they must be very busy, perhaps one of the waiters was off sick. He'd taken off his suit jacket and rolled up his sleeves. Nick delivered the food, and Fran watched while he talked to the people at the table. He paused to speak to those waiting in the queue. He said something, and everyone laughed. Then he went back inside.

He hadn't seen her. He hadn't seen her standing there, on her own, across the street. He hadn't had a chance to wave at her, blow her a kiss, or shout 'Where the fuck have you left the baby?' Fran turned around and started home. Every step she took was a little faster than the one before until, after a few moments, she was running.

Fran opened the door of the flat. Silence. Into his room. There he was, breathing evenly, sound asleep. He hadn't moved since she left. She felt nauseated she was so relieved.

In the sitting room, she noticed the light was flashing on the answering machine. She pressed play. It was her sister's voice. Eight hours time difference; evening in London, early afternoon Vancouver time. She dialed Sarah's work number. Secretary. She waited to be put through.

'Fran! Good to hear from you.'

'You called me.'

Her sister drew a breath.

'How are you?'

'I'm all right.'

Pause.

'How are you?'

'I'm fine.'

Pause.

Fran tried to think of something to say. She couldn't say I need help Sarah. She wasn't about to say I'm going crazy. She didn't say I've lost myself to nappies and boredom and rage and some days it's all I can do to walk down the street, to smile at Louis, to get up, get dressed, to breathe. Instead she said, 'Have you heard from Mum?' But, of course, that question was as bad as all the other things she hadn't wanted to say.

'Mum?'

'Yes.'

'No. Why?' asked Sarah. 'Have you?'

'Don't be ridiculous. You know she doesn't call me. She hasn't called me since— 1990.'

'Don't exaggerate.'

'I'm not exaggerating.'

Pause.

Sarah spoke first. 'We haven't seen her for ages.'

'Oh. Okay. Well—' Fran picked up a cloth and started to wipe

down the telephone cradle — how had Louis' supper got there?
— 'where do you think she is?'

'I don't know. I've tried the usual.'

'Dad?'

'No. Nothing.'

Fran sighed. 'What do you want me to do about it?'

Sarah spoke sharply. 'I don't want you to *do* anything. No one can do anything. I wasn't calling to talk about her.'

'Okay, Sarah. Why are you calling?'

Sarah didn't answer. They both sighed.

'Where were you earlier?'

'Earlier?' Fran paused. 'In the bath.'

'How is Louis?'

'Good. Saying a few words. Ball. Plane.'

'And the Perfect Match?'

'He's fine.' Fran did not have a lot of patience with her sister. They hadn't got along when they were kids and they didn't get along now. Fran thought her sister was too much: too perfect, too clever, too pretty, too successful. She was a partner in a high-flying Vancouver law firm; she skied in the winter and sailed in the summer and was smug, sleek, and bossy. Her life was a series of glamorous dates and first-class business trips to Toronto and New York. She'd never have a baby and wind up stuck at home on her own. 'Sarah, why are you calling?'

'I don't know.'

'Okay,' Fran said, surprised. 'That's okay.'

'Thanks.'

'That's all right. She'll turn up.'

'I know.'

They said good-bye and Fran put the phone down.

What was she going to do now? The evening stretched before

her like a road to nowhere. She tidied the toys, put away the books and magazines that had migrated across the room, straightened the pictures on the mantelpiece, dusted. The flowers that she had put on the hearth earlier in the week had wilted; she threw them away and washed the vase along with a few dishes.

Fran and Nick used to have a cleaner, when they were both working. Anne, Nick's mother, had objected. She was already ill, but still cleaning full-time. 'Why didn't you ask me?'

'I'm not going to ask my mother to clean my flat,' Nick had said, appalled.

'Why not? I wouldn't charge you.'

'That's not the point!'

Now there wasn't any money for a cleaner, although Fran didn't mind. The flat was so small, it wasn't difficult to take care of it. And what else did she have to do during the long hours she spent indoors with Louis?

Fran opened the front door as quietly as she could. Not quiet enough.

'Frannie?'

Her mother's voice. From the kitchen. Sarah was away on a school trip, back tomorrow. Dad was away giving a paper at a conference in Edinburgh. Back Sunday. Tonight was the only night that Fran would be on her own with her mother, Ireni. 'Alone with Ireni' — that's how she thought of it. Like the title of a West End play, a two-hander where the actors shout at each other all evening.

'Is that you Frannie?'

'Yes, Mum,' Fran called out. Without seeing her, Fran could tell that Ireni had been drinking. She was expert at estimating the amount of alcohol her mother had ingested.

There was no avoiding it. Her. She went into the kitchen.

'Where've you been, sweetheart?' Blousy, smiling. Smudged lipstick, warm embrace. It was five thirty: one bottle of wine, or three big G&Ts.

'Oxford Street. With Claire.' She held up her Top Shop bag.

'Oh good. Let's see.'

Fran dutifully pulled out the spangly little top she had bought.

'Very pretty.' Ireni held out her hand. 'Very girly. Sequins. Haven't seen those for a while.' She spread the top out on the table in order to admire it and for a moment Fran thought that was the end of their exchange. Then Ireni began to take off her own shirt, an old once-black, now-grey, cotton turtleneck, baggy with use, revealing her old, once-white, now-grey, bra. To Fran's horror, she picked up the new top.

'Mum—' Fran started, but it was too late, Ireni had already pulled it on, over her head. The top fit her, sort of, except it looked hideous.

'We're the same size!' Ireni said, smiling. 'Where's the mirror? When are you going to wear this, sweetheart? Is there a party?'

'It's yours,' Fran said.

'What?'

'I bought it for you.'

'You did not.'

'I did.'

'Frannie! That's ridiculous.'

'No it's not. Look, it fits you.' Fran remained calm. If she was calm, her mother might stay calm. She turned away and put the empty Top Shop bag in the rubbish bin. She poured herself a glass of water. She picked up her mother's empty glass. Her mother nodded, before sinking into silence, staring down at her own chest as though transfixed by the shiny top. Fran mixed a G&T, a strong one, half a glass of gin, lots of ice, a little tonic, a slice of the lemon that was sitting on the chopping board, and put it on the table in front of her mother. Ireni reached out to pick it up and Fran saw how her arms were thin, puckered, how her face was lined and dry.

'I'll cook us something later,' Fran said.

Her mother nodded, and took a long drink.

Fran woke to the sound of Louis' chatter in the next room. Dee, he was saying. Dee. Although he was beginning to learn words, he still spoke baby most of the time, the tone and intonation uncannily close to adult speech. Sometimes Fran thought it was as though he could speak properly, but she herself was tuned to the wrong frequency. He sounded happy; she would lie in bed until he began to get bored. Nick was turned away from her, on his side, sleeping steadily. He must have got back late; she hadn't heard him. The curtain fluttered softly on the breeze. Outside, the sun was shining. It had been a long, grim winter, grey and cold, no snow, not much rain. It was good to have bright June days, at last; the sun would feed her, give her energy. She would take Louis to the park later.

Nick rolled over. He reached out and pulled her close. 'Mmm,' he said. He smelt of the restaurant: cigarettes, booze, and cooking. Fran eased herself away.

When she went into his room, Louis was standing in his cot. 'Yeah!' he said, waving, incredibly excited to see her, as though he hadn't seen her for days and days. She lifted him out and put him on the floor; he set off running, through the bedroom, out into the sitting room. He took some cars from his box and began to play. Fran got down Louis' cereal bowl. She peeled an orange for him. She got out the stovetop espresso maker. The beginning of another day.

When Nick got up, Fran took a shower. She ironed a linen dress and cleaned her shoes. Make-up. Hairbrush.

'You look nice.'

She smiled at her husband. He and Louis were on the settee, reading a book. Nick stood up and came over to her.

'How's your week been?' he asked.

'Okay.'

'Maybe we should try to get a babysitter this evening, go out to a film or something.'

'You don't want to go out. You want to stay home and go to bed early.'

Nick put his arms around Fran's waist. She leaned back into him. She took a deep breath.

'What's wrong?' he asked.

'I'm — oh, you know what I am.'

'What are you?'

'I'm — I'm tired of having no money. I'm tired of the routine.' Her voice was calm. She was not angry. Fran turned to face Nick. She read his expression. 'I know you are tired too. I'm not saying this to make you feel guilty.'

'But it does — I do feel guilty. I don't know what I can say to make it better for you.'

'There's nothing to say, Nick. I've got to do something. I've got to — do something.'

They had been over it time and again. They had been through the figures: they both ran businesses, Nick had been running Twenty-One for years, Fran had managed Celine's shop for over a decade, they knew about figures. They had tried to find ways to economize, and to a certain extent, succeeded. All their bills were lower than when Fran worked, with the exception of central heating. They didn't run a car. They didn't take taxis. They hadn't gone on holiday since before Louis was born. Their mortgage on the flat was large, but it wasn't worth moving to a cheaper part of London because of the cost of moving, and the added cost of Nick having to travel to work.

'Can you try for more money?'

'Tariq won't discuss it.'

'He doesn't pay you enough.' Fran's voice was flat, toneless.

Nick didn't reply. Fran was right, but there was nothing to say.

It wasn't as though either of them could simply conjure up more cash. Lately, Fran had wondered about asking her father for money; she phoned him once with the express purpose of asking for a loan, but when she heard his voice, and tried to form the words, she failed. She had supported herself since she was eighteen, for Christ's sake, why couldn't she do it now? And besides, she didn't know whether or not her father had any money. She didn't know if he was paying for her mother these days. Asking him for money would have meant asking about that as well — she couldn't face it.

So, after that part of the conversation, Fran and Nick would move on to whether they should go into debt. Take out yet another loan against the flat, increase the mortgage yet again, and use the capital to finance her return to work. But neither of them liked the idea of debt, they were the same in that. You were supposed to work to pay off debt, not take on debt in order to work. That was why Nick hadn't invested in the restaurant when he'd had the opportunity. That was why Fran had never put money into the shop.

They both knew where this conversation led: nowhere. Nick's wage, decent as it was, disqualified them for government handouts. There was no money for childcare. Fran could not go out to work. Fran had to stay home with Louis.

She had not bargained on this. It was not part of her plan. When she imagined herself with a baby, it hadn't occurred to her that she would not go back to work. In the haze of early pregnancy she hadn't considered the detail of how, or when; she had a vague picture of herself, happily at work at the shop, the baby asleep in the corner, everything in its place. In the later months she and Nick began to discuss practicalities — of course she'd stay home while the baby was tiny, not working would be a great novelty, like a prolonged, relaxing, holiday, she'd never not worked in her entire life. But, even then, it had not occurred to her that her leave might become permanent, that she might not be able to return to the adult world of commerce and coffee breaks, that however much she objected (and she didn't object all that much; how could she?) it might be years before she could afford to work again.

'I don't think I can do it much longer.'

'What?'

'This. Louis.'

Nick flushed. His cheeks went pink. He had a tendency to high colour when he was cross, or embarrassed. It was one of the things Fran found most attractive about him. 'What can I do? I don't know what I can do,' he said. 'Some women would love to stay home with their kids.' He regretted it even before he said it.

Fran looked at him. 'Well,' she said, 'I guess I'm not one of them.' She closed her eyes. Nick did not say, What's happening to you? Fran did not reply, I can't do it. It's like I've been buried beneath a huge pile of nappies.

Louis got down off the settee and toddled over to them, holding out his book. 'Book,' he said, 'Mummy.'

'I'll go out then,' Fran said, bending low to give Louis a kiss.

'Okay. Where?'

'I don't know. Newsagent. Café.'

'By yourself?'

She nodded.

'You should call someone. You're always on your own these days.'

'No I'm not. Louis.'

Nick looked down at the child, smoothed his hair. 'Do you need money?'

'Good idea.'

Nick fetched his wallet out of his coat. He gave Fran some cash. Nick didn't begrudge Fran the cash, but both of them couldn't help but resent the fact that he had to give it to her. He went back to reading to Louis.

Fran dumped the contents of her handbag on the counter. From the pile of stuff she removed Louis' toys — a car, a black taxi, and a red double-decker bus. She removed the spare nappy and the wipes and the empty beaker. She swept away the fluff and playground sand that had accumulated and put her make-up bag, her wallet, and the tissues back inside. She went into the drawer and got out her chequebook and her passport.

She left the flat.

Fran walked along the street. Being out in the morning light wasn't as exhilarating as her brief escape had been the previous night, but it felt good to be on her own. She looked at her watch; she had to keep an eye on the time. It was nearly ten; she had an hour before she needed to go home. She stopped at a café and picked up a coffee. Back on the street she spotted a payphone — ditching her mobile had been one of their economies.

'Come round,' Claire said. 'I'm painting my toenails.'

Claire had never left the Fitzgerald family home. There was no reason for Claire to leave. Even though she had plenty of her own money, she couldn't afford a house as big, as comfortable, as convenient, as her parents, 'so,' she liked to say, 'why should I leave?' Her father took early retirement — he had so much money he could make more money by not working — and he and her mother decamped to their house in the south of France. Now there was even more reason for Claire to stay.

When they were teenagers Nick used to say that it was a good thing Claire was rich, because she was so stupid. 'It's natural selection,' he maintained.

'Come on, Nick,' Fran said, impatient with his theory.

'No, listen. Poor people have to be really clever in order to get on in the world.'

'Like you, you mean.'

'Well — yes. While posh people — it doesn't matter if they're stupid. If they're rich, they'll be okay. It's God's way of striking a balance.'

Fran walked west, past the large terraced houses, their façades cream, lavender, pale blue, pink. There were flowers in the front gardens, and the leaves on the big trees were a new, fresh green. This part of west London was so pretty, so well tended, well serviced, well renovated, it made Fran ache with envy. London was such a wealthy place. It wasn't like most cities where there was one wealthy neighbourhood to which the rest of town aspired; in London money was everywhere — Notting Hill, Holland Park, Kensington, Knightsbridge, Chelsea, Mayfair, Hampstead — and spreading, Chiswick, Islington, Clerkenwell. Poor people weren't getting richer, there were simply more and more rich people. They were flooding into London from all over the world, like inverse refugees, the real economic migrants, attracted by the shopping, the restaurants, the private schools, the cachet. Fran knew all about them; they shopped at Celine's in the daytime and entertained each other in Twenty-One at night.

And, of course, poverty is relative. Fran knew that however desperate she felt about her own situation, she wasn't poor. She wasn't poverty-stricken, not by a long way. She just didn't have any money.

She continued weaving through the residential streets until she came out on the main road. Holland Park tube station; Claire lived a little further south, up the hill toward the park. There was a flower stall inside the station. Fran used some of Nick's money and bought six pink and white tulips.

Once she had paid, she turned and found she was standing beside a map of the underground. She traced her finger along the Central Line eastward, into the heart of the city to Holborn, where the red Central Line bisected the deep blue Piccadilly Line, which travelled south and west to Heathrow. All the way to Heathrow. Heathrow Airport. All the way.

Fran paused for a moment.

I've got to do something.

She moved over to the ticket machine. She had the correct amount of change. She punched the buttons and bought a ticket. She had nothing with her, except a bunch of tulips and her handbag.

THE LAKE

They drove up from Vancouver in three cars when they could have all fit into one.

Fran and Nick were in a car they had hired for the week. 'Tin can,' Tony declared when they pulled up with it the night before.

'But it's red,' said Fran.

'And small,' said Nick. He still found coming to Canada a lesson in gigantism: everything was bigger here, including — especially — the cars. He couldn't drive, had never learned; non-driving men were common enough in London but in North America it was like not having a penis.

Fran's parents — Tony and Ireni — were taking the station wagon. It was the family car, like the house was the family house, the only car the family had ever owned, at least as far as Fran could recollect. It was a woody, long and brown with wood-effect panelling along the sides, the interior all done up in cracked brown vinyl. The wide bench seats were perfect for lounging, seat-belt free. On long trips when they were little, Fran and Sarah used to fill up the backseat with pillows and blankets and burrow in with their *Archie* comics.

Sarah was travelling on her own, in her flashy black Toyota.

So, in a three-car-convoy, five hundred miles in one day. 'Shouldn't we stop somewhere for the night?' asked Nick, feigning innocence.

'No!' they all — Fran included — shrieked, 'that's not the way to do it. You've got to drive all the way in one day.'

'That's the way we do it in this country,' added Tony. 'Otherwise you'd never get anywhere, ever. You'd spend your entire holiday driving there, then driving home again.'

They packed up the cars the night before, stepped out of their pyjamas and into their clothes at 5 a.m. and, the woody out front, got up the Fraser Valley before the traffic. At Hope they turned north on the new highway, the Coquihalla, a broad steep path blasted through the granite, up and over the Cascades. At the toll booths beyond the summit they got out to stretch their legs, Tony obligated to complain, yet again, about how much the highway had cost to build, and, without noticing the contradiction, how the ten-dollar toll was highway robbery. Then the Connector across prickly dry high ranch-land, mile after mile of wooden fence-posts, running along beside the road, to where the Okanagan Valley opens up, with its sixty-mile lake, and across the floating bridge to Kelowna. They stopped for breakfast at Smitty's having been on the road for more than four hours.

At the table they sat in silence, staring at the menus, while a young waitress with gleaming red hair filled their glasses with water and ice. Fran's ears were full of the shh-shh of traffic. She looked around the restaurant.

'They are not going to make good coffee here.'

Tony looked up from his menu. 'I saw a coffee place in the entrance to the mall.'

'Will you order me pancakes and fruit salad?' Fran asked Nick. 'Tell her to hold the whipped cream.'

'Whipped cream?' said Nick.

'Yeah,' said Fran. 'They put it on everything. It comes in an aerosol. Spray-on.'

'Oh,' he said, 'okay.'

'We abandoned civilization when we left Vancouver,' said Sarah.

Tony gave her an admonishing look.

'It's true, Dad.'

'We are going to commune with nature,' Tony replied.

Sarah and Fran both laughed. Nick looked alarmed and smiled quickly, as though to reassure himself that it would be okay. Everyone looked at Ireni, but Ireni was saying nothing. During the past week she'd been a vague presence, quiet in the day — 'Hungover probably,' Fran had said to Nick — softly drunk and cosy in the evening. Now she was silent and clearly intended to remain that way.

Fran took their coffee orders and walked across the parking lot toward the mall. It was already hot, that Okanagan dry heat that builds and builds in the Valley all through July and August, the kind of heat that makes pine trees, crackly with dried pitch, explode into flames. Up behind the mall she could see a small orchard on the ridge, surrounded by new housing. Tony had said they should buy some fruit while they were in the Okanagan, peaches and apricots this time of year. 'This all used to be orchard land,' he said when they got out of the cars, but as far as Fran could see, all that grows in Kelowna now is malls. Can you have suburbia, Fran wondered, where there's no urbia in the first place?

After breakfast they moved onto the empty roads of the southern interior, climbing the road-passes over the Monashees and the Purcells as the mountains gained momentum toward the Rockies.

On the downward slopes, the runaway lanes — dirt tracks dug straight up into the mountainside, sand-banked at the top — got steeper and steeper. As a kid Fran had always wondered about the runaway lanes, which she knew were meant for heavy logging trucks with failing brakes: what happened when you got to the top? How would the driver stop the truck from rolling backwards down again?

They bumped along the US border, crossing and re-crossing the railroad tracks. They glimpsed lakes and rivers through the trees, so many lakes and rivers, Fran thought, that surely at least half must be nameless. Every hour or two they drove through a town of sorts — gas station, second-hand shore, fly-blown general store with a roadside ice-cream-cone sign flapping in the tailwind when a car passed by. At Grand Forks two enormous deer stood in the middle of the main road and what traffic there was came to a standstill. Nick and Fran had lost the other cars on the open highway.

'I think Mum grew up around here somewhere, maybe,' Fran said to Nick. The café across the street had a sign in the window: 'We serve borscht and Russian delicacies.'

'Do you want to stop?' Nick asked. It had never occurred to him that Ireni might have come from anywhere other than Vancouver. Fran had never mentioned it before.

She shook her head. 'No. Let's keep going. Once these deer get out of the way.' She stuck her head out of the window. One of the drivers up front had got out of his car and was making large, elaborate, shoo-ing gestures, and shouting.

'So Ireni comes from Grand Forks,' Nick said, looking around at what he could see of the place — wide streets, weeping willows, big old houses on large lots. 'Good name for a hometown.'

'No, no, not Grand Forks — somewhere even smaller, I think. Her parents were Russian.'

'They were?' Nick looked at Fran. He thought he knew everything there was to know about his wife and her family.

His own mother had died before Christmas; a quiet death in a life lived quietly. He realized, not for the first time, how Ireni's drinking had come to dominate everything to do with Fran's family, as though the family didn't really exist, apart from Ireni's drinking.

'So you're a Russian girl,' he said.

She laughed. 'Hardly. They were Doukhobors.'

He looked at her.

'A sect. A Russian religious sect that came to Canada in order to escape persecution.'

'Really?'

She nodded.

'What else?'

'There's no what else. That's all I know. Don't ask her about it. She doesn't like to talk about her family. We had very little to do with them when we were growing up. I only met my grandparents once — twice maybe — when Sarah and I were very small. I don't remember them.'

'Are they dead?'

'I don't know.' She looked at Nick. 'That's all I know. Okay?'

'Well that's weird,' said Nick.

'You think?' Fran smiled. 'Seems totally normal to me.'

West, and farther west still, all the way across the province. Nick stared at the map and saw the long thin lakes that stretched down from the north where the land cracked open between the mountain ranges. He didn't need to help out with navigation; much of the time there was only one road, and they were on it. But he charted their progress anyway, as though to reassure himself that they hadn't taken a wrong turn and wound up in another dimension, a universe that consisted solely of trees.

Fran wondered whose idea this holiday had been. Tony's. She'd agreed to it because she thought Nick would — should? — like to see more of British Columbia. They'd been coming to Vancouver together for years, but rarely left the city. All that Great Outdoors: it was intimidating.

When Fran and Sarah were young — before they'd gone to live in London, before Ireni's drinking had become like a disturbed child, an extra member of the family — they spent several summer holidays at rented cabins, often on Okanagan Lake, one year at Christina. They'd swim all day, and lie in the sun, read piles of books and comics, play cards, and have potato chips and barbecued hot dogs in the evening, Ireni and Tony both relaxed, happy. So when Tony suggested 'a cabin at the lake for a week' Fran thought it sounded like a good idea. The first family holiday in more than a decade, since Fran stayed behind in London when she was sixteen.

At lunch in Trail Sarah said, 'I don't know how much longer I can take this. It's so far. It's so boring.'

Ireni hadn't come into the restaurant. Tony said she was asleep. 'I don't know why you wouldn't come in my car with us,' he said now. 'You could have all snoozed together on the back seat.'

Fran and Sarah eyed each other.

'It's better this way,' Fran said.

'I need my own car,' said Sarah. 'I don't know how long I'll be able to stay at the lake.'

This was news to the company.

'The office might call me back in mid-week.'

Fran suppressed a sigh.

'She's doing so well,' Tony said — of Sarah — to Nick.

Fran nodded grimly. They hadn't been able to find any decent coffee for several hundred miles.

After lunch, through the hot afternoon — only Sarah's car had air-conditioning — over the Salmo-Creston and on to Yahk, hour after hour, Fran rubbing her eyes with exhaustion, ordering Nick to find better radio stations when often there was no radio signal at all, they came upon yet another lake, Moyie, passed a derelict mine on the hillside and spotted the two other cars pulled up in front of a lakeside general store — fly-blown and empty, with a roadside ice-cream-cone sign flapping in the breeze.

'Are we there yet, Daddy?' Fran asked as she got out of the car.

Tony was brandishing a hand-drawn map. 'The lake we're going to is up behind this one.'

Nick had crossed the road and was looking out over the water. It was early evening, seven o'clock, and the big lake was still and flat. There was no noise apart from the tiny sighs of the water. He felt like he was long way away from anything even vaguely famil-iar. He felt his body had been pressed flat by the journey.

He crossed back and climbed into the car. They were in con-voy again, on their epic foray into the continent, the woody out front with Tony and the map his friend Rab, the cabin owner, had drawn for him.

'The water was lapping,' Nick said.

'Hmm?' said Fran; these last few miles were going to be painful.

'The water. It lapped.'

Fran glanced at Nick. They'd left the big lake behind and were climbing again, surrounded by trees, long shadows cast across the road making it dark while the sky was still bright with sunshine. 'There will be plenty more of that where we are going, I'm sure,' she said.

'Good,' he said, 'good.'

'Rub my neck. Please.'

He obliged.

And then, at last, they arrived, Tony waving at them on the gravel road, showing them where to turn down the steep drive. They got out of their cars slowly, like hermit crabs pulled from their shells, and looked at each other, blinking. Turned to look at the cabin. Tony went back to the car to hunt for the door key.

'Where's Mum?' Sarah asked and just then they heard a great splash rise up from the lake.

'She's gone in before us!' Fran shouted and both she and Sarah took off at the same time. They ran all the way down the rickety wooden stairs to the dock, threw off their sandals, and jumped in, fully clothed.

Fran surfaced, gasping. The water was black and frigid. The moon was already high in the darkening sky. She could hear Sarah spluttering on the far side of the dock. Her clothes fluttered around her in the water, touching her and giving her little frights, as though she was surrounded by weeds. She rotated in the water, away from the dock, trying to see her mother. The lake was narrow here — only a hundred metres or so across — and Ireni was a good two-thirds of the way already. 'Come back, Mum!' Fran shouted, her voice tiny against the mass of water and sky. 'Wait for me.' But suddenly the water felt too black and too cold and the sky was almost dark. Up at the cabin, the lights went on, shining down on the water, yellow, inviting. She swam around the dock until she reached the ladder. Climbed up the slimy rungs and found her sister huddled there, shivering in her wet clothes.

'Will she be all right?' Sarah asked, looking toward the sound of their swimming mother, whose dark head was no longer visible.

'She'll be fine,' said Fran. 'She's a great swimmer.' They picked up their sandals and climbed the stairs toward the cabin, leaving wet footprints behind, there for a moment, then gone, evaporating in the night.

Rab's cabin had been in his family for two generations; his father and two of Rab's uncles had built it. In the fifties the family had lived and worked in Cranbrook, the nearest town, but the younger generation — Rab included — had left for Vancouver or Calgary and beyond. Rab's kids were now adults and none of them had much interest in the cabin on the lake in the Rocky Mountains, so in recent years Rab had taken to persuading his friends to visit the place with their families. It was only usable for two months of the year, Tony said Rab had told him — high summer, June or September at a push, although in June the lake was too cold for swimming and in September the ground might start to freeze. The rest of the year the cabin was on its own, left to settle and shift under its great burden of snow.

It was August now, and the lake was warm, at least, the top two inches of surface water was warm-ish. Whenever anyone jumped in they screamed; they couldn't help it, it was involuntary. Except Ireni, of course, Fran had forgotten that her mother was, in some essential way, amphibian. Her bathing suit was old, and baggy on her; her skin had a tinge of grey beneath the tan; in the morning listening to her cough was a painful thing: but when she dove into the water in one long slim slice, she left behind herself, she left behind her disappointed family, she left behind the drink.

They quickly fell into a routine, their days governed by the extraordinary trek of the mercury in the thermometer that hung outside the kitchen window. When they got up in the morning, the temperature would start out very low, zero or just above, three or four at most. Tony would get up first, throwing on a fleece over his pyjamas, and he'd start the fire in the old iron stove in the main room where he and Ireni were sleeping. Fran and Nick, in bed on the porch, blankets, quilts, and sleeping bags heaped on top, talked to each other before getting up for the novelty of seeing their frozen breath on the air. They ate breakfast outside at the picnic table, wearing all the warm clothes they'd brought with them, blankets clasped round their shoulders. But then the temperature would start to rise along with the sun — 9 a.m. ten degrees, 10 a.m. fifteen degrees, 11 a.m. twenty degrees — and by early afternoon the thermometer would be pushing thirty, and they would all be in the lake, the black water a huge relief.

In the mornings they pottered; Tony drove into Cranbrook to get the newspaper, to buy groceries. Ireni went along some days, but this depended upon how much she had drunk the night before, if more supplies were required. Fran took Nick into town a couple of times, but Cranbrook didn't have a lot to offer: there was a good place for coffee, next to the mall — where else? Fran said — but by then they'd got in their own supplies at the cabin.

Mostly they swam, and sunbathed, and read, and ate potato chips and, in the evening, barbecued steaks and hamburgers and played cards, cribbage, gin rummy, hearts. There was no TV, and no radio, no noise at all in fact, apart from the water in the lake, and the wind in the trees. 'Hey,' Nick would say, 'it's lapping.'

Late at night the silence grew noisy. Before going to sleep in their bed on the porch, Fran would lie next to Nick, and listen hard. There were night sounds — the water always moving a little around the dock. There was an owl, somewhere down the lake, and bats that lived in the roof of the empty cabin next door, and other things that crunched and scattered on the woodchip footpaths. They'd hear a loon from time to time. The cabin had no indoor plumbing, apart from the kitchen sink; there was a shower hooked up in the woodshed — lots of spiders, and occasionally, a frog. And, further away from the cabin there was an outhouse, an outdoor privy, a small wooden building with two toilet seats — 'Two?' said Nick, 'why are there two toilet seats?' — and an electric light. Lots of spiders in there too, and other things that scuttled and fled, you hoped, when you opened the door to go inside. Fran found going to the outhouse at night truly terrifying, unable as she was to banish endless replays of *The Evil Dead* and *The Texas Chainsaw Massacre* from her mind. The stinking black hole of the outhouse — the smell was really quite extraordinary — was dismaying enough in the daytime but at night, well, she avoided going out there if she humanly could, if she could make it through without embarrassing herself. Which usually meant she had to go out there at least once every night.

Nick, on the other hand, didn't really mind the outhouse. He liked the way that, if you felt like it, you could leave the door open while you sat and looked down at the lake. And at night, he could see the moon and thousands of stars in the clear dark sky.

There was nothing around to disturb that darkness. Vancouver was hundreds of miles to the west; Fran told Nick that Toronto was at least two thousand miles due east, maybe more, and there was nothing between here and there except Calgary and Winnipeg and they didn't really count, Fran said. Even less to the north, you'd have to go all the way over the Pole and back down the other side before you'd find a decent-sized city. And south, well, just the long spine of the Rockies stretching down to Denver, another thousand miles of lakes and trees.

Sarah's office didn't call her, and they were all tactful enough not to mention it. They found a rowboat stowed under the cabin, a pair of worn, splintery oars tucked beneath the seats, and took it in turns to row up and down the lake. One evening Fran and Nick rowed the boat down to the end nearest the cabin, where the water was weed-choked and full of rotting trees that had been felled by beaver. Fran lay back in the front of the boat and let Nick steer their course; she dangled one hand in the water and felt like Ophelia, beautiful and a bit loopy. It was strange being here, so far from London, with Nick, with her family. She looked back at the cabin. Sarah, Tony, Ireni: and then Nick, with his own parents now both dead and buried. So few of us, she thought. A tiny family.

'Nick,' she said. He was staring intently across the water. 'Let's have a baby.'

'Look Fran,' he said, and he raised his finger to his lips to silence her. He pointed.

There was a moose standing in the water. It dipped its head down and looked up at them, chewing. It was enormous and preposterous, tall and heavy-bodied, with a great long nose and spindly long legs, shaggy fur and huge muscular haunches. As it ate, it watched Nick and Fran; as it ate, Nick and Fran watched it. And then a mosquito landed on Nick's face; he moved to bat it away and dropped an oar into the lake. The moose loped slowly into the trees.

Nick looked at Fran. He smiled. He fetched the oar, and then moved forward, toward Fran, rocking the boat. 'That's why I came to Canada with you,' he said.

'Why?'

'To see a moose. And to get you pregnant.'

Each day, Ireni got worse. She drank more, earlier. She spent more time on the lake, either in the water itself or lying on the dock, sunbathing. She kept a drink with her at all times and somehow the glass was never less than three-quarters full. Sometimes the girls lay on the dock beside her, room enough if the three of them turned over at the same time. They didn't talk, but read or dozed. It was fine with Fran that no one wanted to talk; it was a good way to keep the peace.

One afternoon Sarah dared Fran to swim under the dock, through the blackened and slimy pilings, and out the other side. Fran took up the challenge; neither sister could pass up a dare from the other. She dove under, her heart pounding; it's a mixed blessing of lake swimming that you can open your eyes underwater without being stung by sea salt or chlorine. She was afraid of what she might see — an old tire, a great white shark, a dead body? Instead, she saw a bottle of vodka, swimming from a rope in the cold green water, knocking against the pilings. So that's what her mother was drinking, vodka and lake, no ice.

On Friday morning Tony got up with even more purpose than usual. He threw on his fleece and laid the fire in the stove. From the porch, Fran could hear him moving around: he was cleaning up; she could hear bottles clinking. Although it was early and still cold, and Nick's naked body felt warm and sweet, she forced herself out of bed and into her layers of clothing. They weren't due to leave until Sunday, but her father was making a pre-emptive strike on the mess they had accumulated.

There were a lot of bottles. Fran put the kettle on and watched as her father boxed them up. 'I'll take them into town today,' he said. There was a stack of newspapers and a large bag of plastic milk and juice containers that would need to go to the dump to be recycled. Fran began to lug the boxes up to the woody. It wasn't until her third trip that she realized what her father was doing. He'd finished clearing out the empties and had started opening what was left, methodically pouring the alcohol into the sink.

'Dad?' said Fran.

He looked at her, but said nothing.

He reached for the corkscrew once again, but she got to it first. 'Don't. It won't work. It's not the right way.'

'Give it to me.' Tony held his hand up. 'Fran. Give it to me.'

Fran hesitated.

'You don't know what it's like. You don't have to live with her.' He took the corkscrew from her hand and continued emptying the bottles.

When Sarah and Nick got up, Fran made pancakes from scratch and bacon and eggs and coffee. They sat outside at the picnic table and ate, their faces turned toward the sun.

'Dad poured all the booze down the drain,' Fran said.

Sarah didn't open her eyes. 'He does that.'

'He does?'

'Once every couple of months or so. It's not a good idea.'

'What can we do?'

'What is there to do? We wait. We wait and see what happens when Ireni wants a drink.'

Nick had taken to spending most of his days in the rowboat,

trying to get a closer look at the moose who appeared in the exact same spot at the same time every day, as though he'd been hired. When the moose was not available — on a break? — Nick did something he referred to as 'fishing'; he used a rod and a line and a hook he had found under the cabin, but he had no intention of catching anything. He worked hard at casting and reeling in, took pleasure in the sound the line made.

Nick was already out in the boat when Ireni got up that morning. Fran was lying on a towel on the dock, in the sun, reading a novel about a serial killer; all the books in the cabin were about serial killers, which didn't help much with going to the outhouse after dark. Sarah was in the shade, under the trees, painting her nails. When they heard the shouting all three turned and looked up at the cabin.

A lot of shouting, the words indistinct; Tony and Ireni were inside with the doors shut. It continued; five minutes, Sarah looked at her watch, ten minutes. Ireni's voice alone, for a while, Tony no longer answering. They sat absolutely still as they listened. Nick stared at the fishing line where it met the water; Sarah concentrated on her hands; Fran looked at the print on the page of her novel; they were like small, frightened children once again.

The porch door of the cabin flew open and Ireni ran down the wooden stairs. She was dressed in shorts and a top — most of the week she'd been in either her bathing suit or her pyjamas. She ran onto the dock — Fran rolled out of her way — and dove straight into the water. She surfaced once, and went under again.

The lake was silent. Fran sat up and looked at Sarah. Sarah took off her sunglasses. They were both about to speak, to do something, to say something at last. Then Ireni emerged from beneath the dock, and climbed the ladder out of the lake. She was clutching her bottle of vodka.

Fran and Sarah and Nick watched as Ireni went up the wooden steps to the cabin. There was no more shouting. After a moment, they heard the car door slam, the woody's engine revving. They heard the wheels spin in the gravel on the steep drive. Then Ireni got the car up, and away.

Fran found her father sitting in the kitchen. She could see that he'd been crying. He sighed, and beckoned her closer, pulled her down so that she was sitting in his lap. She put her arms around his neck and leaned into him.

'She's gone,' he said.

'To the liquor store?' Fran half-hoped her father would say yes.

He shook his head. 'Vancouver. She'll turn up at home, maybe next week.'

'She's done this before?'

'She disappears, yes,' Tony said, and from his look Fran could tell that it was already happening regularly, and that Tony was already kind of used to it.

And that was it. Ireni ran away from the cabin at the lake. Ireni got in the car and drove away and no one said a word. They spent the rest of Friday and most of Saturday swimming and lying in the sun. In the late afternoon, Nick and Tony drove into Cranbrook while Sarah and Fran cleared up and packed. The men arrived back at the cabin with a crate of beer, which they stuck in the lake to cool while they fired up the barbecue. All four proceeded to drink. They'd spent the week not drinking much — how could they, Fran thought, in front of Ireni? But now she was gone it was as though they'd made a pact: they were going to get very, very drunk that evening. And they did. They ate potato chips and played cards and did not talk about Ireni. Fran threw up in the kitchen sink around midnight. When they went to bed, Nick put his arms around Fran, Fran tucked her head under his chin, and they stayed that way, wrapped up, limb to limb, all night.

'We are beset by silence,' Fran said to Nick in the car on the long drive back on Sunday. Tony was travelling with Sarah in her car. They'd left the cabin at dawn.

'What do you mean?'

'We can't talk to each other. Me, Sarah, Tony, Ireni — it's like we keep bumping into each other at social events, but we can't remember each other's names. So, yes, we're related. But that's it. There is nothing to say.'

Nick shook his head. 'There's plenty to say.'

'About what?'

'Ireni, for one thing. You just don't know where to begin.'

Fran nodded. 'That's right. Ireni gets in the way.'

'Not Ireni. Her drinking. It creates this big huge black hole in the middle of everything. It sucks out all the light.'

Four days later, Fran and Nick flew back to London, back to their absorbing, absolving, working lives. The police had brought Ireni home the day before, tattered and dirty but oddly sober, contrite even. Tony went down to the municipal pound to fetch the woody. He took the car to the car wash, then drove his daughter and son-in-law to the airport.

Once home, Fran kept in touch with her father via e-mail, brief messages devoid of any real content — 'I'm fine. Nick's well, busy with a refit at the restaurant. How are you?' — phoning on birthdays, Christmas. Ireni began to disappear more frequently.

It was three years before Fran and Nick remembered it had once seemed a good idea to have a baby.

RESTAURANT BABY

By two o'clock on Sunday afternoon, I was concerned. By four o'clock I was worried. By six o'clock that evening — that warm, soft, midsummer evening — I understood that something terrible had happened. Fran was never late. She was never unreliable. She knew I had to go into work for the lunch shift. She knew the clock ticked, the clock ticked loudly.

Claire rang around twelve, when I was just starting to wonder where Fran might be.

'Where is she?' she said.

'Hello, Claire,' I replied.

'She said she was coming round. She still isn't here.'

'Oh. Maybe she got sidetracked. Maybe she's at Celine's.'

'Bugger. I've got to do some shopping. I've got a date tonight.'

'A date? With who?'

'Nick, you're like the horrible little brother I never had.'

I laughed. 'I'm four months older than you.'

'When your wife comes in, tell her that's it, our friendship is ruined, she should never ring me again.'

'Okay.'

'Tell her I'll come round tomorrow evening.'

'Are you sure about that?'

'Well, maybe. We'll see.'

I wished her luck with her date — Claire is perpetually single, no matter who we introduce her to, no matter how many dates she's been on — and put the phone down. Louis had sucked the juice out of his satsuma and was dropping the skins on the floor. Not for the first time, I wished we had a dog. It would make cleaning up so much quicker.

I looked at my watch, Fran was late, and I felt uneasy.

At seven o'clock that evening, I called the police.

'She's late,' I explained.

The officer laughed. 'Give her twenty-four hours, mate,' he said, 'she'll come crawling back with her tail between her legs.'

I had scrambled to provide cover for myself at lunch. Alice, my headwaiter, could handle it. I spoke to Gina, the chef. She was cool; it wasn't like I did this every other day. And now, here it was, Sunday night, the one evening every week Fran and I spent together. I put Louis to bed. After that I sat up, waiting.

I didn't know what to do. I'd already talked to Claire, and when I rang Celine she said that she hadn't seen Fran. 'Why,' she wanted to know, 'why are you asking?' By now I was full of panic and dread, but I didn't want to tell her that. I didn't want to have to tell anybody anything.

In the hours that followed I must have dozed on the settee because I kept waking up, thinking I had heard her come in, thinking I had heard the phone ring. 'Fran?' I'd call out. 'Is that you?' Silence. It began to get light; she'd been gone all night. Had something awful happened to her — hit by a car, abducted by a psychopath? I decided to take a shower, but when I went into the bathroom I found myself with my head in the toilet, throwing up, despite not having eaten. I had no idea what to do.

I put on my shorts and tried to watch breakfast TV. When Louis woke up I changed his nappy and gave him a banana. He said 'Mama?' a couple of times, but he was okay. I put him in front of a video and got out the phone book. I'd start with hospitals.

The phone rang as I reached for it.

'I'm sorry,' she said, 'I'm sorry, I'm sorry.' She began to cry.

'Fran—' my throat tightened, I couldn't speak. Where was she? What was she doing?

'I'll be— I don't know— I'm going—' she was crying too hard to continue.

'Louis,' I said, 'Louis and I—' I wasn't much better off.

We both choked and spluttered for a little while. Louis was looking at me, so I moved into the bedroom. Seeing our bed, seeing her things, calmed me. 'Okay,' I said, 'where are you?'

I could hear her taking deep breaths. Wherever she was, it was quiet.

'I needed to get away—'

'Away from what, Fran? Me?'

'No. Yes. You. The flat. London. My life.' She took another deep breath. 'Louis. It was too much, I couldn't— I'm a bad— I—' her voice was catching in her throat once again.

'Speak slowly,' I said. 'Where are you?'

'I used the Visa… I booked a flight.'

She'd left the country. The floor shifted beneath my feet and I sat down on the bed.

'Where?'

'I can't do it, Nick. I can't be by myself all the time. With Louis. I can't—'

I knew now. I knew exactly why she had left. She'd been telling me for months.

'What the fuck do you think you're doing?' I shouted. 'How the fuck do you think I'm going to manage?'

I slammed the phone down. Then I picked it up again immediately, but I had been cut off. I dialed Call Retrieval but the number was not available. I slammed the phone down once again.

I remember the first time I saw Fran. She was with a younger girl who could only have been her sister, standing in the corridor at school. She looked annoyed. She was dressed very oddly, like a kid from American TV — baggy jeans, a faded t-shirt, and an old plaid shirt over that; the girls I knew were all wearing mini puffball skirts with their Doc Martens that year. It was the beginning of term and their first day; Fran didn't know which classroom to go to. I overheard her say, 'I suppose they're speaking English.'

'The Queen's English,' her sister added, mournfully.

'They don't sound like no farking Queen to me,' Fran replied in what I guessed was her idea of a London accent. The younger girl smirked dutifully.

I decided to intervene.

I thought Fran was exotic; her accent was full of light and air, with all those round Canadian *o*'s and *a*'s. I was tall and skinny and spotty; she was skinny and spotty herself, though not tall. Fran told me later she spoke to two people that first day — I was number two. Number one was Claire Fitzgerald. From that day on, Claire was Fran's best friend and I was Fran's boyfriend. It was as though we had been there all along, waiting for Fran to arrive.

She stopped dressing like that, baggy and American, very quickly. She told me that she made her mother take her shopping after school the first day; from then on it was little black dresses and big boots, just like Claire Fitzgerald. I was sad, I coveted that plaid flannel shirt and, of course, Baggy American became the standard uniform for all teenagers worldwide a couple of years later. But if she had to copy someone's style of dress, Claire was not a bad choice.

Fran and I, I don't know, it worked. It worked then, and it continued working. I think we both felt buffeted by life, as though we were on a continual tightrope walk, about to fall off. We grabbed hold of each other and could not let go. Fran had the whole business with her mother, I think that was a big part of what was behind it for her. And me, I'm not so sure, except I've always been wedded to routine. I've been told this so many times by so many people that I've come to accept it as the truth: I'm not very good at change. I like things to remain the same. I met Fran and that was that, I did not want anything about us to change. I was sorted.

But don't get me wrong, I loved Fran, I loved her then and I love her now, despite everything. Fran is the love of my life. It might sound stupid, maybe even clichéd — how could a fourteen-year-old boy know something like that? But I did. We did. Once we got together we both knew everything would be all right. No matter what happened to the people around us — Fran's mother and the drinking, my parents and the cancer and the dying — we were together, and we were all right.

What happened? Well, Fran's family went back to Canada, and she stayed behind. We did our A-levels. It was the sharp end of the eighties and rave culture was going strong, so we gave up on Fran's old favourite, Kurt Cobain, went to huge parties and danced all night. Our friends were cool but we were not, so at the end of those long nights we were usually sober. We didn't take drugs, we couldn't see the point, we'd rather have sex. We had a lot of sex. Oh yes.

Fran could have gone wild when her parents left London — the Fitzgeralds weren't exactly the most vigilant of guardians — but she didn't. In a way, her rebellion was more subtle and underhanded than that: when she was eighteen years old, she married me.

Finsbury Town Hall on Rosebury Avenue, Claire and her parents, Fran's parents and sister who had flown over specially — Ireni, drunk, Tony trying hard not to show his dismay — my friend Tariq, my brother and my parents: and us. I wore a tie and Fran wore a little hat with a veil that I lifted off her face when it was time. We signed the papers and walked down the road to a greasy-spoon café where we ordered egg and chips and celebrated.

At eighteen Fran was small, dark-haired, and sexy. Even then she dressed well, in clothes that made the most of everything. People — men especially — had a tendency to patronize her, to pat her on the head, to treat her like a child. She'd react with a cool ferocity, a kind of self-assured poise that said, don't mess with me: I may look small, but really, I'm big. She kept her accent, which marked her as an outsider, and she was quick-witted and smart. I found her completely mesmerizing. If I hadn't met her, well, I don't know, there'd be no point to my life. It sounds extreme but that's what I believe.

So, we got married and we worked hard, me for Tariq, Fran for Celine. Sometime later — quite a long time later — Louis arrived. Two people went into that maternity ward, and three people came out. We conjured him up, out of thin air. A little stranger. And things were no longer as easy, as clear, as they had always been.

After I hung up on Fran that first morning, I wasn't sure what to do next. I got Louis dressed. I'd call the restaurant, say I needed a day off. I'd never done that before but I'd never been left on my own with a child either. I needed to calm down, to think. To talk to somebody. We'd go see Claire. We'd take the tube and walk through Leicester Square. That would make Louis happy.

Claire was posh; I was not. Although the school we attended was surrounded by some of the most expensive residential property in London, most people who could afford it paid for their children to be educated elsewhere. I lived on an estate just north of the school; my father worked for London Underground, my mother was a cleaner. Claire lived — still lives — in an enormous house that overlooked the nearby park. Her father was a barrister, from a wealthy family, her mother had lunch with friends; sending Claire to the local comprehensive was the last vestige of her father's youthful fling with socialism. The first time I met him he said, 'If that school was good enough for Tony Benn's children, it's good enough for mine.' Posh people are such wankers, I remember thinking. I smiled politely. Already I was good at smiling politely.

And although Claire is posh and I am not, if you didn't know us you'd think it was the other way around. Over the years my accent has modified; I wasn't aware of it happening but apparently it did. Last year I was interviewed on a radio program about the west London restaurant scene. When I heard the item I thought, who's that posh git talking about my restaurant? and then I realized it was me. People in the catering trade tend to be a bit on the rough side, to put it mildly, and because I'm tall and thin and have cheekbones where other men have chops I sometimes get tradesmen talking to me as if I'm Little Lord Fauntleroy. Claire, on the other hand, has been to the Guy Ritchie School of

Elocution, all wide vowels and dropped *t*'s. She even says 'innit' several dozen times every day.

I'd been to the National Gallery to see Claire often enough in the past, although always with Fran. I took Louis in through the rear entrance and one of the attendants told me where we could find her. She was in Gallery Room 17, standing beside the Titian with her hands behind her back, like a cop. Louis sat in his pushchair and stared at the giant boobs while I attempted to talk to Claire without him hearing.

'What do you mean?'

'She's gone away. I don't know where she is. She flew somewhere. I don't know how long she'll be.'

'What?'

I began to explain again.

'No, I mean, she left Louis behind?' Claire was staring at Louis. She looked as though she was going to cry.

'Yes.'

'What are you going to do?'

'I don't know.'

'Did she say how long she might be?'

I shook my head. Louis was getting restless. He wanted to get out of his pushchair and run through the gallery, smacking the paintings with his mucky hands. He sucked his thumb and, as a result, his hands were always damp. He usually had little wet balls of dirt trapped between his fingers.

'Claire, do you know anything about this? You have to tell me.' How could Claire not know? She's Fran's best friend. How could I not know? She's my wife.

'No,' Claire said, walking over to Louis. 'I had no idea.' She undid the straps and picked him up. If it had been me he would have squirmed to get down, so that he could run away. But Louis liked Claire. He liked her face, which he proceeded to pat gently with both hands. Another attendant arrived to take over and Claire suggested we go to the canteen. As we walked through the galleries, she carried Louis. 'I know absolutely nothing about this Nick. I promise you. Nothing. Okay Louis? Want to have a sandwich?'

Louis was happy to eat. When he finished, he got down from Claire's lap and wandered around the windowless, uncomfortable canteen. This kind of staff accommodation is always so lousy. Bad food, bad lighting.

'It's because of her mother,' Claire said suddenly.

'Her mother?'

'Yes. Don't you see?'

'What's her mother got to do with it?'

'Everything.'

'Oh, so you're a psychoanalyst now?'

Claire frowned at me.

'Besides,' I added, 'Fran hasn't seen her mother for ages.'

'That's just it. Her mother — her fucking useless mother—' Claire lowered her voice, 'does she even know that you and Fran had a baby?'

'Well—' I paused. Did she? Did Ireni know about Louis? How could she not? It was a shocking idea, but it was a possibility. Surely Tony would have told her, would have gone looking for her in order to tell her. 'Do you think Fran's gone to Vancouver?'

'Maybe.'

'Fran left Louis and me, without telling me, without saying one word, to go see her mother?'

Claire nodded but now she looked less certain. 'Maybe?'

I sat back and considered. I had always liked Ireni, despite everything. When I was a teenager she treated me like a grown-up, politely, reserved. She thought that Fran and I were a good thing, and she told me so. So I liked her, which somehow made her condition all the more puzzling, as if likeable women, likeable mothers-in-law, couldn't behave badly. But I didn't think that Fran would go to Vancouver; we hadn't talked about her mum for ages and she hadn't mentioned wanting to see her, not since before Louis was born. It did not seem likely.

Louis was pushing a metal chair around the canteen as though it was a form of transport. The space between the chair back and the seat was like a little windscreen. I thought of my dad driving tube trains. For many years he worked on the Northern Line, seventeen miles long, most of it underground. Louis was beginning to pick up speed. Soon he'd be crashing into things.

I'd say good-bye to Claire and wheel Louis through the museum so we could look at a few more pictures of lovely ladies and stern gentlemen. Then we'd go find a bus to take us home again.

'I don't know, Claire.'

'Well, I'm right. It's got to have something to do with Ireni. But that doesn't make it any easier.'

I had hoped Claire would say, oh, don't worry, she'll be back by the end of the week, she told me all about it, she just needs a break. She didn't. Instead, she gave us both kisses, and we were on our way.

And that day ended without Fran coming home, and the one after that, and the next one as well, and I had to find a way to get on with life, I had to find a way to get back to work, I had to find a way to be.

My son, Louis, became a restaurant baby.

When Tariq found out — it took a few days, but he heard about it, eventually — I told him that all over the world children live in their parents' restaurants. 'Think of Portugal,' I said, 'think of India. Think of Chinatown—'

'You're not fucking Chinese,' Tariq shouted.

'Well,' I said, 'are you going to babysit for me?'

There was no alternative. If I'd had to pay someone to take care of Louis during all the long hours I worked, there'd be no money leftover. At least not enough. What could I do, give up work and live on benefits like a single parent from a politician's nightmare? Uh-uh. No way.

And besides, I told myself, it was temporary. This arrangement, and everything about it, was temporary.

I live in my restaurant. Not literally, of course; I live in a flat with Fran and Louis. But the restaurant is my life, and Fran leaving could not change that fact. Did not change that fact. I was shattered when she left, my heart shut down, and my head exploded into a million pieces, but I had to keep going, had to keep working. The restaurant needed me.

There's a little cubbyhole off to one side of the kitchen, beneath the stairs; you can't stand up in it, and it has a tiny window that was, until recently, sealed shut with a not-so-thin layer of grease. In this little room there is a desk, a chair, and a filing cabinet. This is my office, and I'm fond of it. It is where I do the accounts and the VAT, match the invoices to the delivery notes. It is where I write cheques for the suppliers, keep tabs on the chef's orders for produce, fish, meat as well as the stock inventory, this is where I do the payroll for the waiters and the kitchen staff and check up on last night's takings, this is where I do the work rotas, the wine list orders, this is where I do everything that requires bits of paper. I have a system in place to minimize waste, eliminate potential fraud, maintain quality and consistency. I have a computer, a telephone, a mobile, a hand-held PDA, and a fax machine, and I am capable of using them all simultaneously.

Under my new regime, I'm no longer able to use my office after 7 p.m. This is okay — in the evening I spend my time in the dining room. In order to make room, I pushed the filing cabinet into the kitchen. This required a major reorganization of the kitchen day-storage space and Gina, the chef, wasn't happy about it, but that's too bad. In the place where the cabinet had been I put a couple of big cushions, a folded sheet, and a blanket. Louis would be fine here. Nice and cosy.

Once word got out that Fran had left I was hit by a tidal wave of pity. 'Just ring,' people said, waving their hands, '—anything, anything'. Friends, acquaintances, customers even, people I hardly know. Everyone expected me to fall apart. People expected — I don't know what they expected — it was as though they thought I'd put Louis into care or something, hand him straight over to the social services. Boo hoo, my wife's gone off, I can't cope, men don't do this. Either that or they thought I'd find a new girlfriend, a new mummy for Louis, just like that. Drag someone in off the street.

When we were still at school my friend Geoff's mum died. Geoff was sixteen, he had three little brothers. His father married his wife's younger sister the next day. At least, that's what it felt like. How else was he going to take care of those boys? But me and Louis, we are going to be all right. We are okay.

Tariq says I'm a fool, that any other man would have seen it coming. 'Seen what coming?' I reply. It's not as though Fran was having an affair, it's not as though I was a bad husband, that ours was an unhappy marriage.

'We are happy,' I say to Tariq.

'Then you're an even bigger fool,' he says, 'if that's what you think.'

'But we are,' I insist.

'Women don't walk away—' Tariq hisses, 'when they're *happy*.'

And that's just it, isn't it? Women don't walk away.

I was doing my best not to panic. On that first day, that Monday after she left, while Louis was having his nap — from day one, I knew it was very important not to make additional changes to his already dramatically altered life — I tried to figure out who to ring. I couldn't get my conversation with Claire out of my head so, in the end, I called Fran's sister, Sarah, telling myself I'd do my best not to alarm her. In fact, I'd do my best not to tell her anything, unless of course, she knew where Fran was.

The phone rang a long time before she picked up.

'Who is it?' she said.

I'd forgotten about the time zones. 'Sarah, I'm sorry.' I heard her sit up.

'Has something happened?'

'No, no, it's just… How have you been?'

'What?'

'How are you?'

'You are calling me at five thirty in the morning to ask me how I am?'

'Yeah.'

'Where's Fran?'

'She's not here.'

'Where is she?'

'She's— out.'

'She's out? This is too weird. Why are you phoning me? Is the baby okay?'

'He's fine. He's having a nap.

'So Louis is there, but Fran isn't.'

'That's not unusual.'

'It isn't?'

'Well, Fran goes out from time to time.'

'And she's out now?'

'Yeah.'

It occurred to me then that that's what Tony, Fran's dad, used to say when Fran rang home and asked to speak to her mother. 'She's out right now.' It could mean anything. She's asleep. She's drunk. She's missing. I guess the same thing had already occurred to Sarah.

I didn't like Sarah all that much. She was too bossy. Even though she was younger than Fran, she was forever issuing unwelcome, lawyerly, irrelevant advice.

'Where's your mother these days, Sarah?' I asked.

'I have no idea.'

'Vancouver?'

'Most likely.'

'When did Fran last see her?'

'Oh. I don't know. I'd have to think about it.'

'It's just that—' Should I tell her?

'It was that time you were both here at Christmas. Remember? Three years ago.'

I remembered. That awful night. Christmas Eve. Ireni had turned up in a very bad way. I'd put it out of my head. Not something to dwell on, although I imagine Fran wasn't as quick to forget as me.

Ireni had started to drink when… well, actually, I don't know when she started to drink. But it had begun to be a problem for her, and the rest of the family, before they came to live in London. Fran's father, Tony, had taken up a temporary research post at the University of London. I guess it was supposed to be a great adventure for the whole family; Fran says Tony thought it would be good to get Ireni away from Vancouver, away from her life.

Except London isn't an obvious place to come to dry out. When people socialize in London, they drink. At least, that was the case in the 1980s. Nowadays people tend more toward sobriety; this has been apparent in the bar bills at Twenty-One. But back then, social occasions centred on the pub, the wine bar, the private drinks party, and Ireni slipped right into the groove.

So the family's great adventure turned out to be a great adventure for Fran, who was old enough to pretend she found her mother amusing, and a more ambivalent experience for Ireni, Tony, and Sarah. After two years Tony was ready to pack it in and go back to the safety of his tenured professorship in Vancouver, their own house, their own things around them. 'It will be good for Ireni,' he said to me one day and I could hear he meant 'Maybe Ireni will stop drinking'. Fran maintained that her mum didn't care where she lived, didn't care about anything in fact, and Sarah kept saying she wanted to get back to Canada where people weren't so nasty. 'But nasty is good,' Fran said to me, laughing. We were lying in bed together, in her room. 'We're nasty.'

In fact, Fran and I were anything but nasty; but there was

something about her sister Sarah that made us both feel we were up to no good all the time.

Fran insisted on staying in London. She was sixteen, doing well at school, about to embark on A-levels, and there was me to consider. 'I can't leave you,' she said, she kept on saying. And her parents went along with it. When I think on it now, it does seem a little odd. Her parents left her in London, on her own, aged sixteen, and returned to Vancouver, which is — what? 6,000 miles? — away. Maybe her parents did love her less than they loved Sarah. I know that's what Fran felt at the time, despite the fact that staying behind was her idea. I think she was a bit shocked that they let her stay, when she had expected to be forced to leave. She was almost disappointed. But not quite.

Tony, Ireni, and Sarah went back to Vancouver. Fran moved in with Claire Fitzgerald and her family and, for all intents and purposes, so did I.

I had never taken care of Louis on my own for more than a few hours. Fran and I hadn't spent a night apart since his birth. In fact, we'd hardly spent a night apart since we got together. Once, when things began to get really difficult with Ireni, Fran went to Vancouver without me. It was very short notice, and I couldn't arrange the cover. I missed her so much I felt sick all day, every day. But apart from that fortnight, we were always together.

And since Louis was born, we were together, with Louis.

I was okay on the Dad front. Louis and I got on well, in fact we always got on best when Fran was out; when she was around he preferred her, like most babies. Because of my working hours, the split shifts, I'd spent a lot of time with Louis. I knew how to take care of him. I knew all about nappies and meals and baths and toys. I knew how to make him stop crying, how to comfort him, how to distract him, how to give him his favourite things. Fran and I had always shared household tasks, although I admit that since she had Louis she's taken over most of it. But I was well domesticated and knew how to do the laundry and the hoovering and the rest of the cleaning; I knew how to cook, I could even sew on a button. And I loved my little boy.

But I had never reckoned on doing it all by myself. I had never reckoned on Fran leaving.

And Louis was a little trooper. From the outset he appeared to be profoundly unaffected by Fran's departure. It was as though he thought she was out for the evening, or away for the day, and that she'd turn up anytime soon. Occasionally, he'd say 'Mama?' in that way of his. 'She'll be here soon, Louis,' I'd reply, 'she'll be back soon, you'll see.' Time, and its passing, didn't hold much meaning for him. After a couple of days had gone by — just as he was beginning to notice she really wasn't around, she wasn't returning — his memory of her began to fade. At least, that was my theory, that was what I told myself late at night.

During the day Louis was a small jolt of energy, full of smiles, full of jokes, as if he'd never had a mother, as if she'd never walked away. And at night he became a restaurant baby.

I have a computer at home; I can work while Louis is asleep or watching a video. I am accustomed to using my time effectively, delegating, prioritizing; now I have to be that much more effi-cient. Fran left on Sunday, on Monday I wandered around in a daze, on Tuesday I got myself organized. I didn't know when she was going to come back — it could be tomorrow, it could be next week — but I needed to do some planning, just in case. I decided I would go in for four lunches a week, Wednesday through Saturday. I found a childminder — with this, I was lucky; she was a friend of a friend of a friend down the street — who could take Louis from nine until three those days. She had strict instructions to cut his nap down from two hours to half an hour, forty-five minutes at most, and to make sure he got plenty of exercise. She had a couple of other toddlers that she took care of as well. The first day I took him he was so excited to see the other children he didn't even pause to say good-bye to me. I asked her not to let him watch TV; that way, I told myself, when I needed to stick him in front of a video I would feel less guilty.

By the end of the day he was incredibly tired, she did a good job of that, and after I picked him up, I'd take him to the park for a last big run round. In the evening, I fed him and gave him a bath and got him into his PJs before taking him to the restaurant. While it was still quiet out front I'd get one of the staff to read him a story; there were always plenty of volunteers for that duty. At seven o'clock I tucked him up into the little bed I had made for him beside my desk. I made sure the computer and the phone and the fax were silenced. I plugged in the nightlight. I gave him a bottle of milk and his favourite blanket and his teddy. I said good-night and closed the door.

The first night he went to sleep immediately. He must have been so shocked to find himself shut into that little room that he was too frightened to do anything else.

The second night, after he finished drinking his bottle, he climbed out of his bed and began exploring the room. I could hear him talking to himself, his usual litany of 'dada' 'mama' 'ball' 'plane'. After a while, he began to cry. I went in and found him wedged under the desk. I pulled him out, dusted him off, and gave him a cuddle, explaining that he had to stay in his little bed, that he had to go to sleep. I tucked him in. He smiled. I closed the door.

He shouted 'Mama!'

He shouted 'Mama!' again.

And he began to scream.

He screamed and screamed. He kicked the door. He kicked the desk. He kicked the door again. I turned up the volume on the restaurant sound system and went into the dining room. Out there, you couldn't hear him. Not quite. It sounded like there was a baby crying, very far away. I went back into the kitchen and stood beside the door, listening. Every time I'd think he was finished, having tired himself out, he would start up again. I stood there, holding my breath.

That night Louis yelled for two hours.

And then he fell asleep. After that, it was easy.

I take that back. It was not easy.

I knew that he would get used to it. Children can get used to anything. It wasn't like I was an abusive father or neglectful or — heaven forbid — absent. The fact was that, at night, Louis slept in a small, dark, safe room, with his nightlight and his blanket and his bucket — he had a blue plastic bucket that he insisted on taking everywhere with him, like a kind of little boy's handbag — while outside that room there was the combustive boom and swing of a busy restaurant. Louis slept surrounded by noise and people. From a certain perspective, I would venture he was lucky.

I couldn't stop going into work in the evening. A restaurant comes to life in the evening. Lunch is fine, lunch is fun, but it's the evening when the full drama of a restaurant comes into play. I needed to be there. The regulars needed me to recognize them and say hello, to take their coats, to guide them gently to their table. New customers needed to feel confident that, yes, they had come to the right place. And the staff needed me to watch over them, to be their back-up, their leader. Hokey? Yes. But all part of the trade. All part of what makes Twenty-One succeed.

And I was absolutely strict with myself and everyone else when it came to Louis' bedtime. We went into that little room and, when I thought it was time, I came out and closed the door. Once that was done Louis was not — under any circumstances — allowed out again. I knew from watching Louis and watching Fran handle Louis that if he was allowed back into the restaurant even once I'd never be able to get him to stay in that room again. I knew that the way to cope with, to control, Louis (because, let's be frank, at least half the business of parenting is learning how to control your child) was through constant unchanging, reassuring, routine. This is normal now Louis. Good-night, Louis. I love you. Lie down. Good-night.

It was probably illegal. I didn't know and, for the first time in my life, I didn't care. It was the only way.

Twenty-One was doing well. Given the astronomical overheads, the margins were low, but the place was nearly always full, so the economics were stable and easy to manage, provided I kept a firm grip on it all. Forty seats, no bar; small but streamlined, well designed. Thoughtful.

All my staff are on the books, legal, which is fairly unusual in this trade; some people prefer to be paid cash in hand, but I find it too nerve-wracking, even though the Inland Revenue has never come near us. My honest streak annoys Tariq no end, but he is willing to let me sort things out the way I like, provided he doesn't have to be involved. When we started out we agreed I'd be paid a salary and not take a cut of the waiters' tips; that salary was good at the time but has remained more or less the same.

We grew up together, Tariq and I, on the estate. Tariq is a couple of years older than me, and had already been to catering college when I finished my A-levels. Even then he was a good British Muslim, a smoker, a drinker, fond of Parma ham, saying his prayers in the mosque on Fridays. At the time his big idea was to open a restaurant; while he was still a student he had set up an employment agency for the catering trade, co-opting all his friends. Within a year he'd made a success of that, and sold the business to raise capital for his restaurant. 'None of that Indian shit,' he'd say to whoever would listen. 'Good, posh, English food with a continental twist. Best-quality produce, best-quality meat and fish.' At the time this was an original approach, although now it's become yet another catering cliché. Except, of course, we do it very well.

Tariq knew from the start that I was a restaurant manager; I don't know how he knew, because I certainly didn't. But he saw this thing in me, this ability to control potential chaos, to be organized and orderly, to keep hysterical kitchen staff calm, to charm and flatter our most smug clientele, to surf the successive waves of demand and supply, supply and demand, that a busy dining room can generate. And he was right, it is as though I was born to do it, and I have my doubts about whether I'm capable of doing anything else now, after all this time.

Tariq gave me an opportunity to invest in the business early on but I had nothing to invest, apart from my own labour. Fran and I had decided to buy the flat we'd been renting; raising the mortgage — we were both only twenty — was complicated, and raising further funds did not seem possible. With hindsight, it is apparent that this was a mistake. I figure everyone has to make at least one big mistake in their lives; this was mine. If I had invested, I would have had more control over the restaurant and its future; we could have gone the way of other well-known London establishments — cookbooks, television, maybe even franchising. I would have had a share in the profits that, over the years, have been substantial. But Tariq had his posh restaurant, and that was it, as far as he was concerned. Any surplus is ploughed back into the business, giving the dining room a face-lift every couple of years, improving the kitchen, staff bonuses at Christmas. Once we were established, Tariq was off into other, more lucrative, businesses. He bought back his catering employment agency and from there went on to make a fortune in recruitment. Now he is known as one of the top headhunters in the country. He has several other companies on the go, I've long since lost track, and he doesn't tell me. Tariq does most of his entertaining in the restaurant; he treats it like a kind of upmarket staff canteen, and I know that's been a good thing for Twenty-One, however much it annoys me.

On the Tuesday night after Fran left, Claire came to the restaurant at the end of the evening and helped me get Louis home. We sat up and drank a bottle of wine. We tried to talk about Fran, but there wasn't much to say.

'Why did she leave?' (me)
'I don't know.' (Claire)
Pause.
'Why did she leave?' (Claire)
'I don't know.' (me)
After Claire left, I tried to sleep.

I couldn't sleep. Around 4 a.m. I had an idea. I turned on the computer and went online to look at the record of transactions for the credit card that Fran and I held jointly. There it was on the screen. American Airlines, Heathrow. So she went to the US. Maybe Seattle, en route to Vancouver? Not quite enough information. I dialed the card's twenty-four-hour helpline. After going through all the security questions they told me that, yes, we had purchased a return ticket to Las Vegas.

Las Vegas? Fran had never been to Las Vegas. Not before we met, not since. Neither of us had ever set foot inside a casino, unless you count once, in the South of France, for about ten minutes, and even then it was only to find the loo, after we'd been having sex on the beach. My father disapproved of betting shops — as newlyweds he and my mother had joined the local parish church, and had been steadfast church-goers the rest of their lives — and I'd never felt much curiosity in that regard. Fran and I bought tickets when the lottery first started, but after four weeks of not winning the jackpot, we gave up. So Las Vegas — I couldn't think of anywhere less likely. I tried to console myself: at least she had bought a return ticket.

And so the days went. I knew where she was, or at least, where she had flown, but that was it. I kept checking online, but there were no further transactions. I wasn't about to get on a plane to go and look for her; I had Louis, and the restaurant, to contend with. It wasn't my style to walk away. I'm not a quitter. Not a bolter. But that's the thing, that's one of the things I lie awake thinking about — neither is Fran.

When we were eighteen I went to work for Tariq, and Fran went to work for Celine. Fran was very good at selling clothes. People laugh at the idea that the jobs we do — catering, retail — require any real skill, but Fran was very good at selling clothes. She made people think again about the way they looked: 'You're nice and tall,' to the woman who stooped, 'Great boobs,' to the woman who was two stone overweight. 'Try this,' she would say, handing over the one item that would, indeed, make that short ugly woman look terrific. Before we had Louis I used to go in the shop on my break and sit and watch Fran work, and it made me laugh to see her turn it on. But there was nothing cynical about what she did, nothing calculated: she liked clothes, she liked helping people choose things. She knew how to make her customers happy.

Some evenings she'd come into the restaurant and charm my staff and the regulars as well: on those evenings she was like a little dark star pulsating with heat and light, drawing everyone toward her. But, more often, she'd be quiet. She'd sit there and watch everybody, smiling. That's what she's like. She's like me: quiet, a little shy in fact. Dedicated.

She made me happy. All those years before we had Louis, the whole of our twenties: she looked good, she smelled good, she worked hard, we had a good time, we had great sex, we had everything.

And then we had Louis. And she slipped away from me. I can see that clearly now, from my newly established, lonely, vantage point. It wasn't that he came between us, although of course, inevitably, he did, you have to let your baby come between you, that's the whole point of starting a family. It was more that having Louis seemed to diminish her somehow: she was always small, but she got smaller, as though she was dwarfed by her experience of parenthood. She had to stop doing a lot of the things she loved to do, we both did — the galleries, clubs, films, cafés, shops, the things that London has to offer in lieu of quality of life. She stopped seeing her friends, apart from Claire; our friends from school were divided between those who'd had kids ten years ago, in their early twenties, disappearing from our lives, and those who might possibly get around to having kids ten years from now, when they get closer to forty. And there we were, stuck in the middle, Fran at home with Louis every day and most evenings, while I conducted traffic at the restaurant. It was not perfect. But to me it felt perfectly all right.

The phone rang. It had been four days. A lifetime.

I picked it up.

It was her. She was crying. She hadn't even said hello yet, and she was crying.

'How is Louis? I miss him so much, I—'

Now she was *really* crying. I didn't know what to say. I felt so relieved to hear her voice once again. For a moment: then I began to feel all the other things.

'Oh Jesus.'

'What?' she asked. I could hear her panic. 'He's okay?'

'Yes. Louis is okay. He's fine. He sleeps in the restaurant in the evening.'

'In the restaurant?'

'How the fuck else am I supposed to cope?'

'He would like that. That would be fun for him.' I could hear her trying to convince herself.

'I'm not so sure.'

'But is he okay?'

'Of course he's fucking okay. He didn't curl up and die when you left.'

We had a pause then. We gathered our thoughts.

'And in the daytime?'

'I found a childminder.'

She paused again. I could hear her breathe.

'You found a childminder?'

'He likes it. He doesn't even cry when I leave.'

'How can we afford that?'

'I have no choice.'

'We had a choice before?'

'Yes. We did.'

Another pause. A long pause. The washing machine went into spin cycle in the kitchen. On the coffee table, the tea in my mug vibrated.

'Any new words?'

'Sure.'

'What?'

'"Sure." He says it like that — sarcastic.'

She laughed.

'I say, "Come on Louis, eat your carrots." He looks at me and says "...Sure..."'

She laughed some more. I'm shocked to find how much I love hearing her voice.

'Oh Jesus,' I said, 'Fran. Are you still in Las Vegas?'

Silence. Then the sound of her starting to cry again. It was all I could do not to hang up. 'What are you doing Fran? When are you coming back to us?' To me.

'I don't know. I'm not — I don't know. I need a bit of time. I need to think things through.'

I hear: but I am coming back.

'Oh fuck you Fran, make up your fucking mind.'

'I know you're angry, I know you—'

'I'm not angry.' I was shouting. 'I'm coping. Louis and I are coping. We want you to come back Fran. We want you to—'

'I'm not ready.'

'What the fuck do you mean you're not ready? What's ready got anything to do with it? What are you doing? Have you left me? Have we split up? Should I file for divorce? What is this Fran?'

'I haven't left you Nick,' she said. 'I don't want a divorce.'

'What do you want Fran? Eh? What the fuck do you want?'

Silence.

'When are you coming back to me?'

The tunnel up ahead looked very dark. I was sitting on my father's lap; he was driving his train. I was five. We were deep underground, on the Northern Line. The thin light from the train's headlamps was eaten up by the speed, and the tunnel ahead looked too narrow for us to squeeze through; I kept ducking my head, burying my face in Daddy's uniform. A tiny beacon appeared, far in the distance. That's the station, said my dad, and the light slowly grew bigger and bigger, until whoosh, we were rushing through the bright station, too fast, I thought, we can't stop. But stop we did, and the conductor's voice barked out of the little speakerphone dangling next to my father's head.

A year later, 1975, my father was involved in the terrible accident at Moorgate. He wasn't on the train that sped up instead of slowing down, ran through the sand drag and crashed into the buffers; he'd have been killed along with the forty-three others who died. I don't know where he was when it happened, what he did to help. He never spoke of the accident, at least not to me, but he came home from work late that day. My brother and I were having our tea when there was a knock at the door. My mother opened it and screamed. There was a black man standing on the landing. This was not odd in itself, and it took me a minute to realize that my mother was screaming with laughter and took me even longer to figure out that the black man was my dad. My mum stopped screaming soon enough when my father continued to stand in the doorway, not moving.

'Where's your keys?' said my mum.

My father didn't answer. He blinked, slowly.

'Are you auditioning for the minstrel show, love?' my mother asked. When he didn't reply, she turned to my brother and me and told us to go to our room. We got down from the table and watched as she led my father by the hand to the bathroom.

It was soot from the fire caused by the crash. He'd been blackened from head to foot, like a piece of burnt toast. I forgot about it, soon enough, the world of grown-ups was full of strange surprises. But my father did not take me with him to work again.

I think, after Moorgate, he was afraid. Afraid of the Northern Line, the black tunnel, its seventeen long miles. But that fear, which came to him at night — sometimes I'd hear him shout out in his dreams — didn't keep him from working, didn't keep him from taking care of his small family. He was a union man, and he worked on the Underground all his life before retiring early, already ill with cancer. He used to tell me he was a lucky man and that he'd led a lucky life. 'I'm a lucky fella,' he'd say, then he'd grab me and rub his hands on my belly and my back before hugging me hard. 'Stop it, Daddy!' I'd shout. And he'd say, 'But Nick, I'm rubbing my luck off onto you.'

Was my father lucky? He spent thirty years underground and when he came up for air, he died.

I've had a different kind of luck than my father. Twenty-One; Fran; Louis. There was no reason for my luck to change.

These days, if I am truly lucky, Louis will have slept through the night. He's prone to nightmares now; maybe that's what keeps reminding me of my father. He shouts out like he's seen a monster, but when I go to him, he's asleep. 'Night terrors,' one of the mums said to me at the playground the other day, but I'm not so sure. I think Louis wakes up crying because his mummy has gone away. But, on a good night, he won't wake. He'll sleep through and wake up in his cot in the little room next to mine and he'll talk to himself for a while, baby chatter, the odd real word enounced with peculiar clarity. I'll lie there, half-listening, dozing. Then he'll get bored and it will be time to start our day.

Breakfast for us both. Dishes into the machine. I'll get Louis dressed, and get out some of his toys for him to play with while I shower, shave, iron my shirt. It's amazing how quickly time moves in the morning, we nearly always run late. Louis into his jacket, me into mine, a couple of favourite toys into his knapsack and I pick up my bag into which, hopefully, late last night I stuffed everything I'll need today. Down the stairs, Louis holding my hand — they're steep and he's still not quite up to it on his own — out into the street. Louis has to walk. Either that or I carry him. I've abandoned the pushchair. I can't stand the fucking thing. It reminds me of Fran, although she would hate that — of seeing Fran coming along the pavement toward me, pushing Louis. It's so awkward and large and unwieldy. He walks, I hold his hand.

The childminder lives around the corner. We started out with a 9 a.m. drop off, but after a couple of days I had to move it to 8 in order to get a jump on the morning. One of the other kids is usually there already, and Louis totters off without looking back at me, as though he's been going for years. I have a quick chat with Julie; she's always very professional about this business of taking care of my child, she's never taken it upon herself to quiz me about Fran and her whereabouts. She didn't know Fran, although they must have seen each other in the playground. As far as she's concerned Fran never existed, it's always been just me and Louis. And that's fine. That's easy.

Back down the street in the direction from which I came, past the flat, which is handy because I often remember I've forgotten something, some vital bit of paperwork, along past the organic supermarket and the gallery and the antique shop and the jeweler and the newsagent, all the way to Twenty-One.

I unlock the door, let myself in. I bring in the post, and any deliveries that have been left outside — the milk generally, not much else, most suppliers come along a bit later in the morning. Then I lock the door behind me.

The restaurant smells — of wine and beer and cigarettes, and of cooking. Frying, grilling, deep-frying, roasting. Fish, meat, chips — these are the things that linger. All restaurants smell in the morning. I once went to talk about a job with an acquaintance of mine from the trade; people offer me jobs fairly regularly. He was a manager at The Ivy, and we arranged to meet there first thing in the morning. When he unlocked the front door and led me into the dining room the first thing that struck me was the smell. Even The Ivy stinks, I thought, of stale booze, cigarettes, and day-old cooking. The frontage of Twenty-One is glass — sliding panels that can be opened up all the way during warm weather and, above these panels, windows. Using the long handle I open these and then I go through the kitchen and open up the back door in order to create a through draft. I turn on the big Italian coffee machine.

I go into my office, push Louis' nest out of the way, and start in on the paperwork. Last night's takings, invoices, wages. I get the computer to print out the stock inventory. There are frequent interruptions; the suppliers start to arrive. Some suppliers come once or twice a week — dry goods, for example, the cheese specialist — and others, like the wine merchant, come less frequently. But some come every day: the butcher, the veg people, and the fishmonger. These are the ones you have to keep your eye on; it can be difficult to find suppliers who are absolutely trustworthy. I've got a good eye, but even so, when the butcher says his organic pork loin came in from the slaughterhouse last night, I'm going to have to take him at his word. I'm going to have to trust that it isn't, in fact, week-old chemically enhanced pork loin that he hasn't been able to sell to his other, bigger, venues, that when he says the slaughterhouse he doesn't mean that big freezer they keep out back. I'm fanatical about shellfish — we only serve it when I can be absolutely certain of its quality. And the veg, well it has to glisten and crunch.

I spend a lot of time on the phone sourcing our supplies. I

want our raw ingredients to be of the highest, freshest quality. As well as the suppliers who arrive at our back door, I also get goods by mail order. Truffles straight out from under the boar's nose. Wild mushrooms direct from the forest. Raspberries so ripe and fresh that when you touch them, they bleed.

And then there's the wine. I could easily spend a day a week researching, sourcing, and ordering wine. Our wine list is one of our real strengths: eight whites, eight reds, two champagnes, one sparkling white and, in summer, two rosés, every bottle of exceptional quality.

As the suppliers arrive, I check the deliveries before signing for them. Then it all has to be put away in the day fridges or in the basement where we have more capacity for storage. Usually by now Gina will be in as well and she'll be hard at work with her *mise en place*, her basic prep. She's very methodical, and the kitchen work stations are highly organized, everything within logical, convenient reach; the bull's eye — a flat stainless steel cooking surface — next to the *bain marie*, next to the deep-fat fryer, the grill above the bull's eye, the plates warming beneath the *bain marie*. Before she does so much as chop an onion she makes sure that the equipment is clean. We alter our menu seasonally; if Gina had her way she'd change the menu every day, but I think in a restaurant like ours people prefer stability; they have their favourite dishes that they order time and again, and they're disgruntled when they disappear. So, like I said, we change the menu according to seasonal variation, but these changes are over and above the day-to-day menu. We have asparagus when fresh asparagus is ready in spring; we have game — partridge, grouse, and venison — in autumn.

The morning is when I might call the carpenter or the

plumber to come in to take care of any minor repairs that need doing. If there's a problem with last night's rubbish collection — and there often is — I'll call the council and sort it out. If Gina or I have left something out of one of the orders, or if we had an unexpected run on a particular dish last night, I'll grab a taxi and head over to the cash and carry. If one of our chairs has been damaged I'll take it over to our chair supplier, where I can have it fixed, maybe pick up something new for the kitchen while I'm there, replace a bit of equipment that is no longer up to it. The wear and tear on the restaurant and everything within it is substantial; sometimes I'm amazed that the very fabric of the building isn't wearing thin from the numbers of people, the throng and hubbub that passes through.

By the time I get back, everybody else will have come in for the lunch shift, the two waiters, Greg the *chef de partie*, and Roman the KP. The waiters will be busy laying the restaurant, polishing the windows as well as the cutlery — I like to do the glasses myself — straightening the pictures on the walls and making sure the dining room is spotless and ready, and the KP will already have a large pile of washing-up to get through. The waiters take it in turn to clean the loos throughout their shifts; they know that the state of the loos is very important to me. Dirty toilets in a restaurant, I can't think of much worse. They're all smokers — everyone who works in the trade smokes, except me — and so they need to have their fag breaks before we get going. At 11:30 Gina will produce a meal for us — again, this varies according to the weather, the season — but it's usually something light, salads, bread, pasta. We sit down and eat together, Gina included, and this is when we talk through menu changes or shift problems, that kind of thing. We know each other pretty well, and rely heavily on the symbiosis that comes from working long hours together. And our lunch — however brief — is a vital part of the day.

By twelve we might even have our first customers. And off we go, whether or not we are ready. Now is when my real work — the business of keeping everyone happy — begins. And this is what I'm good at, keeping everyone happy. This is what I do best.

With one obvious exception, of course. Fran. My wife.

VIVA LAS VEGAS

Where do you go when you want to disappear? What kind of place will embrace you? Where can you go when you do everything badly, when nothing you've started has gone the way you planned, when you're about to let yourself — and everyone around you – down? When there is one thing, one, single, enormous thing, that you are expected to do, to be, in fact, but you can't do it, you can't be it, you're no good at it? Where can you escape to when you have nothing left? Where's the place you've never been, the place you've never had any desire to go?

Fran looks up at the banks of monitors that show departure times. Trolleys laden with luggage flow through the terminal entrance behind her, like a river swollen by the incoming tide. She calculates she'll need ninety minutes to buy a ticket, check-in, and get to the gate on time. Ninety minutes; she scans the monitor screens looking for the right place to go. There it is. She sees it, she sees her destination.

Las Vegas. Las Vegas, Nevada. A place she's never wanted to go, a place she has never been.

I didn't mean to leave. I didn't mean to leave the neighbourhood, let alone the country. But when I stood in front of that tube map in Holland Park Station, and had the idea of getting on a train, then the idea of going to Heathrow… I had to sort myself out. I had to go away. I needed time, I needed to be alone, away from my life, away from Nick and Louis. It made perfect sense to me, at that moment, on that day.

And it was easy. I bought the ticket. I went through to the departure lounge, I walked down the long corridors to the gate. No one stopped me. No one said, 'Excuse me, Fran, but what do you think you are doing?' I showed my passport and my boarding card and got on the plane. I took my seat. I fastened my seat belt and sat with my fellow passengers, as placid and unmoved as they appeared to be.

Then the plane pulled away from the gate. And I woke up, as though from a deep and dreamless sleep. 'Oh my god,' I said, loudly. 'What the fuck am I doing?' Everyone within ten rows turned to stare at me; the woman in the next seat stifled a scream. They all watched to see what I would do next. I was near the emergency exit — what would happen if I undid my seat belt and went toward it? Would that big man across the aisle get up and tackle me? Would the airhostess attempt to restrain me? Would I be arrested and taken off the plane in chains? Oh my god, I thought, what am I doing?

As the elevator moves down the tower toward the casino floor the noise grows. When the doors slide open, the noise envelops her, and Leslie moves through it swiftly. The slot machines with their banging and whizzing and trumpeting, all those women seated firmly in front of their quarter, dollar, five-dollar, here at Caesars they even have five-hundred-dollar machines, the coins chinking in their tubs, the silver clanking as it is swallowed and — occasionally — spewed by the machines. Leslie walks through the inferno until she reaches the relative peace of the card tables with their soothing green-felt tops, the dealers calm behind them. She walks around until she sees a free place at a table she likes, twenty-five-dollar minimum per hand, a dealer she doesn't know but recognizes. She's not fussy about which seat she takes, she doesn't care where she comes in the order of cards, she's not a card-counter. Leslie is not a superstitious player; she doesn't believe that a bad player can take 'her' cards away from her. She puts ten thousand dollars — one hundred hundred-dollar bills — on the table while the dealer deals to the other players. The floor manager jumps over to the table like the grasshopper he was in another life.

'Hello, Ms Sinclair, how are you tonight?'

Chandeliers, black waistcoats, and bow ties.

'I'm fine, Fabio, very well.'

The manager speaks while watching the dealer change Leslie's money into chips. 'Is it cold up in Canada?'

She laughs. Fabio always asks this question. 'Not at the moment. It's summer there too.' She gets the dealer to break the chips down so they're all twenty-fives.

'Play well,' says Fabio, nodding and smiling. 'Let me know if I can get anything for you, Ms Sinclair.'

But before Leslie can get started, before she places her bet, the all-important first bet of the trip, she sees her. The young woman she met at the airport this morning. She was wandering around outside the baggage carousels, like the ghost of a package deal, clutching a battered bunch of tulips wrapped in florist's paper. One of Leslie's bags had yet to come through and she was beginning to get impatient, thinking that they might have lost it; she looked at her and felt an unexpected pang of worry, and then she looked away.

Next thing the young woman was standing beside her. Who is she, Leslie wondered, why has she come over to me? The young woman spoke first. 'Where are you from?' she asked.

Despite the location, this felt like an odd question. Leslie thought her accent peculiar, unplaceable. 'Vancouver.'

'Oh,' she smiled. 'That's where I'm from. Originally. I live in the UK now. London.'

Leslie had noticed before that Brits tend to call Great Britain 'the UK'. Who can blame them for dropping the 'Great', she thinks. It's an embarrassing way to describe such a small country.

'Can I help you?' Leslie asked. She didn't want to talk to this woman, she didn't even want to be polite, but she couldn't help herself.

'I've run away from my baby,' the young woman said.

With that, Leslie's heart froze, and she turned and walked away.

And so now, when she sees her standing on the far side of the blackjack table in the middle of Caesars, Leslie is not pleased. She looks exactly the same as she did at the airport — same clothes, same handbag, same pale face, as though one gust of desert wind would blow her away. The tulips no longer have any petals, just broken green stems and naked stamen.

And the young woman has spotted Leslie. She walks up to her, as though she's been waiting for her to arrive.

'Hello,' she says, and Leslie can tell she is nervous. 'We met earlier, at the airport. My name's Fran.' Her smile is unconvincing.

Leslie doesn't want to tell Fran her own name, doesn't need to tell her. But she does. 'Leslie. Leslie Sinclair.' She leaves her stack of chips on the table in order to secure her place — this is the right table, after all, the perfect table for her to start her play — and stands up in an effort to deal with this conversation, to get this conversation over and done with and out of the way. 'Well, Fran,' she asks, 'what brings you to Las Vegas?'

Fran looks around then, as though to say, oh that's where I am. She looks back at Leslie. 'I thought it might be a good place to come if you haven't got any money.'

Leslie knows it is true that in Vegas casinos are open twenty-four hours, all day, every day. Leslie knows it is true that in Vegas you don't have to go to sleep. But just because a casino is open doesn't mean you can simply live there, availing yourself of the services, snacking on the peanuts at the bar at night, napping on a lounger by the pool during the day. The security guys — they are everywhere, standing beside you at the poker table, in the ceiling above the slot machines, behind cameras, listening in with their devices — will soon spot you and you'll be on your way out, if not on your way to jail. Fran will last a little longer than most, Leslie thinks; she is female, good-looking, and her linen dress, although spectacularly crumpled, is obviously good quality. She even has on a nice pair of kitten heels. But they will see through her sooner or later, and she'll be on her way.

Leslie wants to get away from her. 'Look, honey,' she says, 'Vegas is the last place you should be if you haven't got any money. Vegas is where you come when you want to throw your money away.'

Fran's expression doesn't change. Blankly trusting and distracted, simultaneously.

I need you, Fran thinks, I need you to help me.

'Fran,' Leslie says, and she knows she will regret it, 'where did you leave your baby?'

Fran looks at Leslie. She smiles, but the corners of her mouth turn downward involuntarily and tears well up in her eyes. And, in that moment, Leslie sees that Fran is a nice young woman to whom something has happened, for whom something has gone horribly wrong. When, at the airport, Fran said 'I've run away from my baby,' Leslie's instinct was to flee. But now that she's facing her again, standing in the casino, looking pathetic, Leslie thinks of herself as a mother and she remembers a thing or two about that time.

Who doesn't want to run away from their children, Leslie thinks. Show her a parent who isn't ready, even for a tiny moment that comes and goes in the space of a sigh, to head for the hills, driven out of their own house and home by a wailing — perhaps whining? — unhappy child, and she'll show you a Stepford Wife. It's not the child's fault, Leslie knows that, children are children, they need our full attention. But they say that when a child is murdered the killer is, nine-point-nine times out of ten, a member of that child's own family. And when Leslie thinks of Charlotte, her sweet, curly-haired, funny little girl, even Leslie, in the midst of her grief, can remember the times Charlotte drove her crazy. The times she wanted to — longed to, begged David to let her — get away. She took four months off work after her girl was born; four months far, far away from her supercharged sales pitch of a life, four months of a two-inch-long tear in her perineum and a hideous bout of mastitis, and she was so ready to go back to work when the time came she would have agreed to a ninety-percent cut in her rate of commission.

Nobody suggested that, luckily, Leslie thinks.

So, without thinking, without waiting for Fran to find a way to reply, Leslie caves in, she caves in completely. 'Listen,' she says, 'I'll buy you supper. You can tell me all about it.' And she sighs heavily, defeated by her own good nature.

'Thank you,' says Fran, 'thank you so much.'

Leslie sees the relief flood into her body, across her face, and that somehow makes her feel even more annoyed with her own magnanimity. 'But I've got things to do first.' She looks at her watch. 'I'll meet you here at ten.'

Fran nods.

'Oh, and you should get rid of those tulips.'

Fran looks down at the flowers, frowning. Then she steps away. And Leslie, at last, at long lovely last, sits down at the black-jack table.

I knew when I got off the plane that I'd have to find someone to help me. I had nothing — no money, only the credit card that I'd used to buy the ticket and that I didn't want to use anymore, not wanting to add extra debt to Nick's worries. I stayed at the airport for a while, trying to figure out what to do, with a vague idea that if I smiled nicely someone might offer to help me. That didn't work, so I got on one of the hotels' free shuttles.

The long flight had dulled me, dulled my panic and dulled the guilt that had roared up to overtake me as the plane made its way down the runway. I drank a couple of gin and tonics and several little bottles of white wine and now, in Las Vegas, I felt drunk, hungover, and jet-lagged all at the same time. They say when you fly it takes a while for your soul to catch up with your body and I had left my soul a long way behind, in London with Nick and Louis.

So when I saw Leslie Sinclair again in Caesars Palace, I decided it meant something. I could tell she was an honest person, a good person; after my years in the shop I was adept at reading people. Clothes do give a fair amount of information, and hers were neat, utilitarian, and chic. I heard her speak and she had a clear, even voice, and I saw from the label on her bag that she lived in Vancouver, so she was a Canadian. And I really did need someone to help me.

After her recent years of custom this casino knows Leslie — or rather, Leslie's credit rating — well. At only twenty grand a pop — lately it's been around eighty grand a year — she is not a real high roller, but they take her custom seriously. They offer her endless hospitality, RFB as they say, room, food, and beverage, plus the occasional massage, pedicure, or whirl in the gym, the odd airport limousine. Once a year they fly her down at their expense, to special events, tournaments, parties, big concerts. Leslie enjoys this, getting to see Barbra Streisand overcome her stage fright. She knows it's sad but for her a big part of the pleasure of gambling is recognition from the casino, and this comes in the shape of invitations, freebies, and obsequious floor managers like Fabio knowing her name. It makes her feel important. Even though she knows full well it's simply corporate hospitality.

She starts off betting low, low for her, fifty dollars per hand, long departed are the days when she would cling to the minimum. There is a man on the far end of the semicircular table, talkative. He is talking to the cards, into his drink, to the table at large. 'I don't know,' he says, looking at his hand, 'Where do they get this shit?' He glances up and catches Leslie's eye. 'Excuse my French, ma'am.'

The dealer sweeps the chips away. Leslie places another bet, the dealer deals another hand. Her nametag says 'Carol — Alabama'. She has one of those sixties beehive hairdos that exist only in Nevada, like prehistoric birds surviving in the desert, extinct elsewhere, but alive and well here, mutating in fact, due to all the atomic testing. Like a lot of dealers, she has long fingers and well-kept nails. Leslie looks at her cards, a pair of sevens against the dealer's up-turned six of hearts. She places a second bet, and the dealer splits the pair, and then deals her two face cards, so she's happy. This is all done in silence.

The man at the end of the table has a pair of sevens as well. He places a second bet, and splits the cards himself.

'Never touch the cards,' the dealer says in a clear voice with a southern tinge. 'Never.'

'Fuck,' says the man. He looks at Leslie. ''Scuse my Chinese.'

The floor manager, who had wandered away, is suddenly there again. 'Don't touch the cards,' he says, in his low voice. Menacing. Leslie laughs, and Fabio frowns at her. She reminds herself to tip him later, make up for it.

'You take my money,' says the man, '*and* you have a thousand rules and regulations. We don't stand a chance, do we?' He looks around the table as if he expects his fellow players to rise up and proclaim him their leader. Instead one man scoops his chips into his baseball cap and gets up from the table. That leaves Leslie and two young men who look like Ivy League students. They stare at the man at the end of the table, their eyes flickering toward Carol the dealer and Fabio the floor manager. This guy is slowing down the action. They are not happy with his behaviour.

'Okay,' the man says, raising his hands in a gesture of resignation. 'I won't touch the fucking cards.' He looks at Leslie. 'Ma'am,' he says, 'pardon my Spanish.'

Leslie sits at the table for four hours solid. In Vegas she finds time has another dimension; it moves quickly, all the familiar markers of the day — light, dark, clocks — removed, and that's part of why she likes it here. She no longer has a past and the future is on the table; there was no divorce, there was never a child. Time is marked by the passing of the dealers — here they work fifty minutes on, ten minutes off, onto a new table, regular as soldiers. Beehive leaves, a young woman with long red hair arrives. Red hair leaves, a crinkly man pushing forty, outdoors type, arrives. Usually the dealers are good at conversation. And Leslie likes to get them talking, to hear their stories; in Vegas everyone always has a good story about how they ended up in a white shirt and bow tie dealing cards from behind a table. But today, the first day of this particular trip, this dark trip to Vegas where it is always night, Leslie doesn't feel like talking, she can't help but think about Fran, Fran who has left her baby. Her mood leaks onto the cards and no one who joins them speaks much either, least of all the linguist at the end of the table. They are united in their pursuit of good cards. The Long Island Iced Tea, syrupy with alcohol, keeps coming. Leslie tips the waitresses and dealers at regular intervals. Toke, Leslie knows she should say; in Vegas tips are called tokes. In fact, there's a whole other language here. A 'nickel' is five hundred dollars, a 'dime' a thousand dollars. 'Comps' are freebies, a 'grind joint' is a casino for low rollers, of which there are plenty. She doesn't use these words, she never has, they make her feel self-conscious, like an impostor — she figures those words are for guys. She tips Fabio the floor manager as well. And at the end of her stretch she has done all right. When it pleases her she's a hard and aggressive bettor and she comes away having lost only five hundred dollars. As she walks across the carpet the chips clank against her hip reassuringly. The good thing about Las Vegas is that, no matter what outlandish concoction they build, no matter how far the casinos expand across the desert, it never really changes.

She has a snack in one of the casino's cafés, out back, near the pool, and then goes to her room and gets changed for a swim. It isn't true that it's always nighttime in Vegas. Indoors, yes, outdoors, well, you'll be in trouble if you step out thinking it's dark when in fact it is 120 degrees Fahrenheit in the shade, if you can find any. This is the other thing Leslie does in Vegas, as well as gamble: sunbathe. She's as unrepentant about sunbathing as she is about gambling. She does it, she likes it. A nice young man from the hotel places a lounger in the sun for her, and she puts on the minimum amount of sunscreen that she can get away with. She orders a drink from a gorgeous young waitress wearing a little white toga, and settles in with a good novel — she prefers Patricia Cornwell and Elmore Leonard but, sadly, they don't write as fast as she reads — and after only a few minutes she can feel her skin begin to fry. She turns over and bastes at regular intervals, orders more drinks and, when she has to, takes a dip in the colonnaded pool, floating past the splashing Neptune fountain. Caesars wouldn't be Caesars without all the columns and pillars, she thinks to herself, without all the modish Greco-Roman charm. As the evening draws on it does not begin to cool off, it never cools off in Vegas in the summer, that's why Leslie likes to come this time of year. But the pool area has begun to empty out, and so she gathers together her things. She misses the babble of the people and the children and the cell phones, and so she heads back into the hotel where she is bathed with casino noise and frigid, conditioned air. In her room she has a shower and inspects her tan. Nine o'clock, she's got one hour before she has to meet that young woman. Fran. She retrieves her chips from the room safe and goes back down to the blackjack tables. In the corridor she runs into a bevy of old girls. One is wearing blue lamé and all four are carrying little shiny gold handbags that they must have picked up back home in a sale. They are very excited, thrilled to be out on the razz in Las Vegas. As they pass, their enthusiasm rubs off on Leslie.

Las Vegas wasn't like I thought it would be, although I'm not altogether sure I'd ever actually thought about Las Vegas. It was bigger, and uglier, and managed to be both spectacular and bland at the same time. The shuttle from the airport took me to Paris and I wasn't surprised to find it was nothing like Paris, France, nor even Paris, Texas, but more like Paris, McDonald's, or Paris, Burger King. I left there and continued wandering, through the long day and into the night, accompanied up the escalators and down the long moving sidewalks by great hosts of people who were also roaming from casino to casino as though looking for something, I'm not sure what, pausing to gape before moving on again. It was hot, and everyone walked slowly, but somehow the oppressiveness of the crowd, and the neon, and the road jammed with tourist traffic, made me feel as though I was floating, as though if I allowed it, my arms would float away from my sides, and my feet would lift off the ground, and I'd be up in the air, on my own, weightless, unencumbered, free. And I wouldn't dare look down and I wouldn't dare look back because I knew what I would see: Nick, standing there, holding Louis.

After finding Leslie in Caesars I wandered over to the Flamingo across the street. The elaborate pink neon façade was familiar from a dozen movies and already I'd seen enough of Vegas to realize that the Flamingo casino had something that most other big casinos had eliminated — daylight. Windows. Doors open onto the street. There I found an older woman — mid-sixties perhaps — decked out in a pink Versace tracksuit and layers upon layers of gold jewelry. She was sitting in front of a slot machine, with an enormous plastic bucket of coins on her lap. She was chain-smoking cigarettes and drinking rum and Coke and the waitress kept bringing her more of both. And she was winning steadily, the level of coins in her bucket getting higher and higher. After a while she looked at me, standing there behind her. She put four quarters into the machine next to hers and said, 'This one's yours.' She pressed the button, the cards came up, and I won ten dollars. 'Parlay?' she asked and I nodded because I didn't know what she meant, and thought for a moment she was speaking French. She whammed that ten dollars back into the machine, pressed the buttons in a sequence, and out came fifty dollars. 'Beginner's luck,' she said, handing me my own bucket so that I could scoop up the coins. 'You can change it into real money over there,' she said, pointing at the cashier across the way. 'Don't spend it all in one place.' She cackled, like a kind of pink witch, and I took that as my cue to be on my way.

The casino is busy this evening. All the blackjack tables are full, so Leslie wanders around to see if there's a floor manager she knows on duty. Before she can find anyone, they open up a new table. She takes a seat. When she retrieves her chips from her purse — in Vegas she uses her larger handbag — a couple of women who are sitting at the other end of the table look at her neat stacks and sigh. Nine thousand five hundred dollars in chips, half her bankroll, less the five hundred she lost this afternoon. Because it is evening, and she is wearing high heels and her little black dress and feeling like Sharon Stone for one glorious nanosecond, she decides to play for five hundred dollars per hand. The women down at the other end are betting the minimum, and feeling every penny. She wants to give them a thrill, show that not all girls stick to the bottom line.

She loses three thousand dollars right off the mark, in less than ten minutes. Sometimes when she comes to Vegas she loses her entire bankroll the first time she sits down at a table. That tends to coincide with the times she's got off the airplane already drunk and gone straight to the tables before checking into the hotel. Losing twenty thousand dollars in a couple of hours is, as the Americans say, a learning experience. Leslie thinks everyone should try it at least once. It gives you an enormous sense of power and privilege. This is my money, you are saying, and I am rich enough to dispose of it in this soulless and useless manner. That kind of losing streak inspires a certain awe — in the loser, and in those watching. A crowd gathers. The dealer commiserates. The last few chips — she might break down and exchange the five-hundred-dollar chips for hundreds, maybe not — are especially poignant. She always wins a little back before losing it all, even more magnificently — splitting, doubling down, playing hard. When she gets up from the table people applaud. The floor manager sets her up for dinner and she spends the rest of the weekend wandering around Vegas, drinking, doing tourist things. Once she's gone bust she doesn't try to extend her credit. It's one of her rules in life.

So she loses three thousand dollars straight off the mark, and then she begins to win it back again. The ladies at the other end of the table cheer up and start asking the dealer questions. The dealer is talkative, and happy to give lessons while taking their money. That's one of the good things about Vegas, Leslie thinks, it is an open place. You can sit down at a blackjack table without a clue how to play, and the dealer will explain it to you, talking through the odds, detailing the house advantage, telling you how to play, giving you his own personal theories on how to win. It's not secret, there are no secrets, and people need to know how to play, otherwise, what's the point? Women find the card tables particularly intimidating, that's why they prefer the slots. At the tables your mistakes are public, everyone can see how badly you play, and a lot of women prefer the ringing solitude of the machines where they can sit in splendour with their tubs of coins, happily throwing their money away. Not Leslie.

Leslie likes Las Vegas because here no one interferes with her. People talk to her, that's okay, she talks back to them. But no one hassles her. She can do as she pleases. If she wants to sit in front of a slot machine all day, then she sits in front of a slot machine. If she wants to drop ten thousand dollars in one afternoon's blackjack, then she does it, even if it's just to impress the floor manager, even if it's just to ensure that the free drinks, the free rooms, the meals and shows and limos keep coming. She knows how it works. She knows how to play.

And it makes her happy. Sitting in her little pool of light, upright in front of the green baise, with her drink and her chips neat in front of her, it doesn't matter, nothing matters, the world could stop for all she would notice or care. Some people might say this is a bad way for a woman to spend her time, her money, but she says, what difference does it make? She doesn't like to shop, she doesn't care much about clothes, she's not into interior decorating. She doesn't have a sailing boat or a cabin on one of the Gulf Islands or a condo at Whistler. She's not interested in leisure time. She doesn't travel, except to come here. She doesn't do any of the things that people with money do. She doesn't even have a family anymore. So she comes here, and she loses money gambling instead of spending it on elaborate toys and hobbies. She comes to Vegas; Vegas is her recreation.

And she still gets a thrill out of being here. She still can't believe that when she sits down at a table, the drinks are free. Who cares if she loses five thousand dollars between placing the order and receiving the drink? That drink was free. The lights, the twenty-four action, the fine balance between glamour and seediness, the hordes of bulky Midwesterners in their shorts and t-shirts — the fact that this place is all about money, money, and nothing else. Who can make it, who can lose it, who can win it. Vegas is capitalism stripped naked, Leslie thinks, it's a big party in the midst of an even bigger environmental disaster. It's like hell, but without the eternal damnation. That, Leslie thinks, will come later.

Her only regret is that she started coming here so late in life.

She wishes she'd come when she was eighteen. She would have been a showgirl, a short showgirl, but a showgirl nonetheless. She would have shown her tits and worn feathers and danced in every revue. She would have retired at twenty-nine and gone into real estate here instead of Vancouver.

In fact, this is the only thing about Las Vegas that Leslie doesn't like: the town is crammed full of real estate agents. It's a boomtown, it's gone from desert watering hole to big city overnight, and everybody who lives here is involved in property development. In Vancouver, Leslie is a real estate agent. In Vegas, she's a gambler, a real gambler, not a speculator or a developer like she is at home, but a gambler. Someone who is willing and able to put their cash on the table, and lose it, and enjoy it, and then leave. She comes here to get away from realty.

Leslie had a drink in Cleopatra's Barge while she waited to meet Fran. She'd managed to claw back some of the money she'd lost, then she lost that, won back some more, and ended up a thousand dollars down. She was happy. There was a lounge band playing songs from the seventies, an ugly period in American rock music. All those white brothers — the bearded Doobies, the blond Allmans, the even blonder Edgar Winters — and their horrible cranked-up songs. Couples were dancing despite the crap music, the men loose-limbed and overweight in their open-necked shirts and tight jeans. She hoped Fran would be on time.

There was a man in a tartan suit (a tartan suit!) looking her way. A conventioneer, Vegas is always full of conventions and conventioneers, whatever the time of year, he looked like a window salesman or maybe bathroom fixtures, was about to lurch in her direction and ask her to dance. He was probably perfectly nice, but Leslie tended to agree with her friend Barbara who always used to say, 'Those guys are nice when they're at home in Spudsville, not when they come to Vegas.'

The tartan conventioneer was unsteady on his feet. He was swaying back and forth, back and forth, as though working up momentum to launch himself her way. Leslie figured he was nearly ready to move in when Fran stepped in front of him, neatly cutting off his trajectory. She couldn't help but smile and Fran thought she was smiling at her.

'Hello,' Fran said. She held out her hand and Leslie took it, thinking, why am I being nice to this woman? Can someone please remind me?

'It's incredibly kind of you to invite me to have supper with you. I've never done this before. I'll pay you back, I promise, it's just... I am... it's temporary. Thank you so much. I—'

'All right,' said Leslie. 'You can tell me all about it.'

As they left the lounge Leslie looked over her shoulder and waved at the tartan conventioneer. He gave a huge smile, hitched up his trousers, and returned her wave.

They headed across the Appian Way into the upmarket Italian restaurant that is part of Caesars vast acreage. (There is no apostrophe. Caesars is ritzy, Leslie says, but not that ritzy.) The restaurant has an extraordinary cantilevered copper ceiling that, after a few drinks, becomes confusing; it's like being trapped inside a big orange House of Mirrors. The food was good though, and it was one of the places where the casino comped Leslie. As Fran looked around, Leslie saw, again, that she was nervous. Leslie wondered, again, what she was doing, giving up perfectly good blackjack time.

They sat down. Leslie ordered wine. Fran perked up a little once she'd had a glass.

'So,' Leslie said, straight to the point, 'where's your baby?'

Fran frowned. Am I ready to talk? I don't know that I'm ready to talk about this. She smiled. 'I won fifty dollars from a slot machine!' she said. 'A woman gave me a dollar to get started.'

'Beginner's luck.' Leslie didn't mean to be sour but she couldn't help it.

'That's right. I'm going to parlay it into some big money.' She laughed.

'Parlay,' Leslie said. 'Okay.'

They ordered their meal. The waiter's nametag read, 'Shawn — South Korea'.

'Talk.'

'Pardon me?'

'Come on. What's your story? Why are you in Las Vegas?'

'I— well— I—,' where to start, wondered Fran, what to say? 'I'm thirty-two years old. I'm married— to Nick. He's a nice man. We have a child— Louis.' She pulled her wallet from her handbag and opened it to the photo of Louis. She had taken it on the day he was eighteen months old. He had curly blond hair and blue eyes and he was holding up a half-eaten apple and laughing, with the sun in his eyes.

'He's darling,' Leslie said, and she thought, I can look at pictures of other people's children now and not feel a thing.

'Yes,' Fran said, and she smiled at the photo before putting it away. 'I take care of him. Full-time. I used to work. I used to have a job. It was only a job, it wasn't, you know, a purpose to life, a vocation, saving mankind or whatever. It was a job.'

'Most people have jobs. Vocations, like vacations, are few and far between.'

Fran didn't laugh. 'I ran a shop. A very nice, small, posh shop. I sold clothes. And jewelry. People asked me advice on what to wear, how to wear it. People — women... some of them were very large,' she smiled, 'and some of them were very small.' She paused. 'I wanted them to look beautiful. And they did. I put a lot of thought into it, and into how the shop should look and feel. It wasn't a social service, people would spend hundreds of pounds on things they didn't really need, on things that, in fact, did not actually suit them. But I felt as though I was doing something, in some small way. People liked my shop. They bought things and felt happy.' Fran stopped.

'You worked in a shop.'

'I liked it. I loved it. I loved my boss, Celine. I loved the street we were in, I loved the big horse chestnut tree that grew across the street. I loved walking to work, picking up a coffee on the way, and settling in for the day, hoping I would have lots of business, hoping I would sell lots of things.'

'Oh,' Leslie said, 'I understand that feeling.'

'And when I closed the shop at the end of the day, did the takings, tidied the stock, swept the floor, I felt as though I'd accomplished something, I'd made some kind of contribution — I even thought it was good to pay taxes, you know, to make a wage and to pay my way.'

'What happened?'

Fran didn't answer.

'I don't mind paying taxes either,' Leslie confessed, and it was true; sometimes Leslie thought she should pay much higher taxes than she did, given the amount of money she made, but she wasn't about to go as far as to say that.

'I couldn't work anymore,' Fran said eventually. 'I couldn't— Louis—' she sighed. 'Childcare. Too expensive.'

Leslie nodded.

'And it is driving me crazy. And I was getting worse and worse, and more and more unhappy, and I couldn't talk to anyone about it, and I couldn't talk to Nick, and there was no way out of it, and I had to get away.'

'Oh,' said Leslie. 'Okay. You needed a break. You came to Vegas to get away. I can relate to that. I'm almost disappointed,' and she sat back in her chair thinking, I can relax now, it's okay.

'Except I ran away. I didn't tell Nick I was leaving. I didn't tell anybody. I didn't know myself, until it was too late. And I really don't have any money.'

The food arrived and, for a while, they ate without talking.

'How about you?' Fran asked, eventually. 'Do you come here often?'

Leslie laughed. 'Oh honey, that's a long story. Another time.'

'Have you got kids? Married?'

Leslie shook her head. Once upon a time in Vancouver. I had a little girl Charlotte. She died.' Leslie took a big gulp of wine from her glass and poured herself some more. She drank a lot in Las Vegas, while at home she didn't drink much at all. She found it interfered with her working day, left her feeling foggy. She used to drink when she and David were fighting, and after Charlotte died it was difficult not to pour a glass of wine as soon as she got home from the office in the evening. Charlotte wasn't there, Leslie wanted her to be there, and usually David wasn't there either, and she would have preferred to be somewhere else herself, in the grave with Charlotte. She would have liked to blot it all out with alcohol. 'I drank a lot after that,' she said, looking into her glass. 'I could have been a world class alcoholic, I'm sure, but something in me resisted.'

'My mum drinks,' said Fran.

'Does she?'

'Yeah,' Fran replied and Leslie watched as she did that thing again, smiling while the corners of her mouth turned downward, blinking hard to stop herself from crying.

'Okay,' Leslie said, 'that's enough for now, enough True Confessions,' and she pushed the conversation on to other things: Vegas lore, Vegas glory. Later, when the meal was nearly finished Leslie thought, I should have told her to go home to her child. I should have insisted, there and then. But it was too late, and, truth be told, they were having a good time, swapping tales of their selling lives, Leslie and her houses, Fran and her clothes. How to find the perfect fit; people who look and look but never buy; how to keep your customer happy.

A little while later they made their way back into the casino, through the crowd, up way past bedtime. The casino was packed; all the tables were open. Leslie had drunk too much to play black-jack, although that wasn't about to stop her. Fran grabbed her by the arm and said she wanted to go back to Cleopatra's Barge. That sounded like a terrible idea, even though, in theory, Leslie was fond of that cheesy lounge bar stuff that Vegas purveys as its idea of cool, as if the Eagles were still — had ever been — groovy. However, Fran was determined to get up on that dance floor, she hadn't had a dance for ages, and Leslie felt compelled to follow her lead. The band had warmed up considerably since earlier and was now doing passable Abba covers. The dance floor wasn't very big and it moved independently of their feet; it really was a barge of sorts, a kind of Greco-Roman pirate ship, floating in actual water, and the whole area smelled of chlorine. After a while Fran waved Leslie over to a table. Leslie gulped her drink down and then had one of those epiphanies that happen after a certain amount of alcohol; the barge began to spin as well as rock. She felt as though she was going to throw up. She was not a vomiting drunk — she used to leave that to her ex-husband David who puked every time he had more than two glasses of red wine. The music was very loud; she had to shriek to be heard. She told Fran she needed some fresh air.

'I'll come with you,' Fran replied.

It is difficult at the best of times to find your way around a casino. The floor space is massive — at that moment Caesars was the equivalent of two football fields — and they build extensions every couple of minutes. Everywhere are ringing bells and flashing lights — there are very few doors and no exit signs, no markers of any kind. Leslie had got to know Caesars well over the years, well enough to negotiate the floor, when sober, by skirting around the walls, ticking off landmarks as she progressed. Drunk, this became more difficult. But she knew her way to the ladies toilet. The air was not fresh, but she washed her face and thought about her hair and re-applied her make-up, and felt better. Fran did the same. My little shadow, thought Leslie.

When they re-emerged she headed in what she believed was the right direction to get back to the drinks. But in between the washrooms and Cleopatra's Barge lay an outcropping of blackjack tables. Leslie circled around; although it was nearly 2 a.m. the tables were still full. She stopped at a table where the players were betting high. She decided that's where she wanted to be. She stood for a while and watched the play, Fran at her side. Blackjacks were appearing with unusual frequency and the table was boisterous and articulate, as though they were playing craps instead of twenty-one. People were winning — nobody was going to get up from that table.

She turned to look further afield.

'Leslie,' Fran said, 'I'm tired.'

'Uh-huh,' Leslie said, nodding, wondering if a seat at that other table had come free.

'I'd like to go to bed.'

'Uh-huh,' she said, preoccupied by the proximity of the cards.

'I need to sleep. I was on a plane all night last night. Do you think I could — would you mind if I…'

'Oh,' Leslie said, finally getting it. She was surprised by the relative directness of Fran's request — surprised enough to capitulate. Why not? The room was huge; it had two queen-sized beds. Besides, it would get her out of the way. She dug around in her handbag, the chips slipping through her fingers like little fish. She handed Fran the plastic key and said good-night. Then she turned toward the blackjack table where, miraculously, a seat had come free.

I don't know how I did it. I don't know what made me think it would be all right. Leslie was drunk, and you could say I took advantage of her, but she knew what she was doing. I'd done this enormous thing of running away; after that, nothing seemed real, everything else was easy. Asking strangers for help — that was nothing. And besides, I was tired. I was incredibly tired. I had nearly two years of tiredness bottled up inside of me. I needed to sleep.

Being in Las Vegas is like being in a movie. A crap movie, but a movie nonetheless. It's not real. It's the most unreal place in the world. Everything about it — from the palm trees to the dealer's smile — is fake. Real, but fake. Imported. The whole city is a set. When you're there, you're the star in your very own movie-of-the-week. That's why Leslie likes it.

She knows that behind the scenes there's a real town out there, a place as mundane and graceless as any other American city, with its shopping malls and second-hand car dealers, trailer parks and dentists and divorce lawyers. There are poor people who can't get ahead — maybe a few more of those than is the norm: there are rich people who can't help but make more and more money — perhaps a few more of those as well. And then there's Leslie, and all the other people like her, the shifting mass under the bright sun, translucent apart from the shiny currency in their pockets. They might think they're stars, Leslie thinks, but really, they're walking, talking, bragging, boasting, winning, losing, dollar signs.

And Fran did not belong here. That was clear from the outset. Leslie still didn't understand why Fran had chosen Las Vegas. People come to Vegas for a reason, even if it's as simple as: to have fun. But Fran, well, sometimes it felt to Leslie as though Fran came here so they could bump into each other.

Leslie was not particularly softhearted. She was not civic-minded, in fact that was one of the things she disliked about living in Vancouver, everyone was so damn full of civic pride. She gave money to charity, primarily to an AIDS hospice; she got involved with that when her friend Gordon, one of the lawyers she used to work for, was dying. She wouldn't dream of handing money to beggars, to street people, the homeless, the crazy. There are volunteer services, as well as entire governmental departments, devoted to taking care of those people. Leslie felt too little, too afraid to take her wallet out of her handbag in the middle of the street. But with Fran, Leslie thought it was different. Fran needed Leslie.

That first night, when Fran said she was tired and Leslie handed her the key to her room — she didn't know why she did it, but she did. There Fran was, she had no money, and she needed to go to sleep. There Leslie was, she had a handbag full of chips, and there was a spare bed in her room. It was as though Caesar himself was encouraging her to take in strays.

So that night she gave Fran the keys to her room. And she went on to gamble.

The key to success at blackjack is being able to add quickly; it's amazing how many people can't add at all. Leslie was good at adding — five of hearts, seven of clubs, three of spades, dealer showing a face card, hit me baby — and, even though she was horribly drunk by then, she kept her wits. She bet low, twenty-five dollars a hand. Despite the small sums involved, and the amount she'd had to drink, the play was as riveting as always. 'What is it about blackjack that makes it so damn interesting?' she asked the table in general. No one replied. She wondered if she'd said the words out loud.

When the waitress came round Leslie asked her for a large glass of water, lots of ice. The play was not going well for her. She was losing steadily, although on twenty-five dollars a hand it was not exactly hurting. The players at her table sat silently. It was the time of night in the casino when people look as though they are playing cards in their sleep. They tend to lean heavily into the table, women rest their breasts and elbows on the buffer, men keep their hands close to their chips so that their movements are minimal. Nobody yawned, and beneath their silence they were alert, but it was as though someone — the Las Vegas Sandman perhaps — had gone around and sprinkled sleep dust over their heads. Leslie thought of Fran, upstairs in her room. The atmosphere was almost cosy.

When the doors of the lift closed, the noise from the casino — all that ringing and beeping and clanging — was blunted; as the lift ascended, I listened to the noise fade away. The corridor was thickly carpeted, hush, hush, hush, said my heels as I walked along. There was no one around; someone had deposited a room service tray outside a door, but the half-eaten hamburger was odourless, as though the smell had been absorbed by the hotel's muffled quiet.

I let myself into the room using the key Leslie had given me. It was a large room; there were two beds as well as a seating area with a couple of armchairs and a settee. There was an elaborately wrapped fruit basket on the coffee table. Leslie had unpacked her suitcase and put her clothes away. Someone had come into the room and turned down one of the beds, leaving a single Belgian chocolate on the pillowcase. I put my handbag down for the first time since I left my flat in London that morning. I poked around the room, opened all the drawers and doors; big TV but no minibar, no Bible.

The bathroom was shiny and luxurious. I hadn't been in a bathroom this clean, this well ordered, for a very long time. The towels were white, thick, in a neat stack on a chrome shelf. There were bottles of hotel-supplied moisturizer, bath salts, conditioner, and shampoo. The bathtub was large and round with Jacuzzi jets, there was a separate tiled shower with a glass door, and the toilet was in its own cubicle. There was a telephone on one wall, a hairdryer, and a white-towelling bathrobe hanging from the back of the door. And mirrors. Spotless, well-lit mirrors. I glanced at myself, and then looked away. I didn't want to see myself. I didn't want to have to look at myself, didn't want to think about where I was, what I had done; I didn't want to think about anything.

There were no toys in the bathroom. There was no changing table and there were no nappies — no piles of clean nappies waiting to be used, no bags of dirty nappies waiting to be taken away. There were no dirty clothes on the floor. I could sit in here for hours and no one would bang on the door, no one would stand outside roaring 'Mama!' The bathroom was a silent chamber within the silent hotel room. Sepulchral. In here, there was nothing except clean tiles, hot water, and peace.

After a while, I ran a bath. I put my dress on a hanger and watched the steam relax the wrinkled linen. I rinsed out my knickers and my bra. I washed my body carefully.

I didn't have anything to wear to bed. I hung up the damp towel and wrapped a fresh one around myself. I'd sleep in the other bed, the one that hadn't been turned down for the night. I climbed in. There was a telephone on the bedside table.

I rang home. I spoke to Nick briefly. He hung up on me.

And then I fell asleep.

Fran waited for her little sister Sarah outside school that day. She wasn't sure why, but she had a bad feeling. They never walked home together, if they could avoid it. And next year they'd have a whole year where they wouldn't be able to walk home together, because Fran was going to secondary school, in the opposite direction. But today, she waited.

'Okay?'

'Yeah.'

They walked side by side, without speaking. Fran could tell Sarah had the same bad feeling. When they got to the house, they went around the back, up the steps to the deck. The back door was ajar. Holding hands — when was the last time they held hands? Fran couldn't remember — they went inside.

The kitchen was wrecked. The cupboards had been emptied onto the floor. Broken plates, smashed glass, torn cookbooks, overturned chairs, open bags of flour and sugar, spilled breakfast cereal, squashed fruit; on top of it all, the sink had overflowed and everything was soaked.

'Oh,' said Sarah after a while, 'they're all right.' She was pointing at two tins of tomato soup that sat, undamaged, in the mess. 'Where do you think Mummy is?'

'Upstairs,' said Fran, 'asleep.'

'She must be tired,' Sarah said, nodding.

Fran bent down and picked up the tinned soup. Sarah went to the utility closet and got out the broom. They began to clean.

Over the next few days, Fran and Leslie moved into a time zone all of their own. Theirs was the simplest of routines: sleep, cards, cocktails, eat, sun, cocktails, cards, eat, cards, sleep, cocktails. Sleep, cards, cocktails, eat, sun, cocktails, cards, eat, cards, sleep. And on it went. Three days. Four days. Fran's routine didn't include cards. Nor all that many cocktails. Some days it didn't include sun either. Instead, Fran's routine included weeping; it included bouts of nausea brought about by the physical pain of missing Louis; and, most of all, it included feeling guilty. Why had she left? Why was she not, at that very moment, right then, at the airport, getting on a plane? In fact, Fran spent most of her time lying on her bed in the hotel room, staring at the ceiling. From time to time she admired the shiny bathroom. Once in a while, she looked out the window at the pool area below and beyond, to the desert hills, faintly visible through the traffic pollution and the dust from the many and vast casino building sites. The room was heavily soundproofed and air-conditioned so, of the world beyond the door, she heard and smelled nothing.

Mostly she was transfixed by the quiet. Mostly she was amazed that she could lie there all day and no demands — absolutely no demands — were made of her. There was nothing to do. The routine was there was no routine. Instead, there was an absence. And that absence was huge. It pushed on her chest like a heart condition, like an unwanted pregnancy.

She made occasional excursions, into the casino, out onto

Las Vegas Boulevard, but she knew right away that Vegas wasn't really her kind of town. It was not a place she understood. But this suited her, it suited her condition, it meant she did not have to engage with it. It meant she could continue doing nothing. Thinking. Leslie left her to it, and Fran was grateful.

And Leslie. It suited her, this arrangement. It made her feel — this was hard for her to admit, even to herself — it made her feel less lonely. And feeling less lonely made her realize that she'd been lonely in the first place.

Fran knew this state — their mutual being and nothingness — couldn't last. She could feel it already, the spell was going to break and they would both be forced awake. What would she do then, she wondered? Leslie would have to go home to Vancouver one day, and then she'd be on her own, by herself in Las Vegas. She needed a plan. She needed to make a plan. But plans were beyond her, alien.

In the shiny bathroom, Fran stared at herself in the mirror. I've forgotten who I am. Who am I?

When was the last time I saw my mother? Christmas, three and a half years ago, before Louis was born; she was in a bad way. And that was it, that was the last time. I did not see her when I was pregnant. She was not there to hold my hand when he was born, she did not come to see me with my newborn baby. She has never met Louis. Her only grandchild. Her eldest daughter's child. My child. Louis.

It would be different if she were dead. It would be different if she were gone from the world instead of simply absent, there but not there. My father, Tony, came to London for two days on his way home from a conference when Louis was three months old. My father's only visit, and even then he was in a hurry to get back to Vancouver, back to the now-always-absent Ireni, 'just in case she comes home.' And yet, he showered love on the baby during his brief visit, he surprised me with the softness and joy he showed Louis; he spent hours walking with him propped up against his shoulder, patting his back when he fussed. But my mother did not come to visit; she didn't even phone, and I didn't ask Tony if she had been told about Louis. Just in case he said, no, your mother doesn't know about the baby.

And now, Ireni doesn't know I've run away.

I raised the white flannel and ran it down my neck. The hotel soap was silky and smooth. The water was hot; there was a pile of thick white towels waiting for me. Once again, no one knocked on the door. Once again, no one shouted, 'Mama!' I took note of the quiet, just as it occurred to me that I had almost stopped noticing.

I wanted to phone Nick again. I'd rung him twice since leaving, and the second time, yesterday, all I did was cry. I wanted to phone him now. And I wanted him to put Louis on the phone — he probably wouldn't talk but at least I could listen to him breathe. But I didn't call. I had no way to pay for the calls I'd already made — they would go onto Leslie's room bill — and, besides, I knew that talking to Nick would confuse me further, that on hearing his voice I'd feel too full of guilt and longing to continue to stay away. And I needed to stay away. I wasn't getting any closer to figuring out why I left, but I knew I needed to stay away. So I didn't ring. Instead, I stayed in the room. And I talked to Leslie.

While Fran looks at herself in a mirror at Caesars, Ireni wakes up under a canopy of tall cedars. The trouble with the Great Outdoors, she thinks, is that it rains too much. Vancouver would be a fine place to live if it wasn't for the infernal rain.

This morning it hasn't rained, but she's soaked anyway, bathed by the saturated morning air. Under the trees, everything is moist, always. She's a hundred yards or less from the sea; she can hear it and smell it. In the distance there's the sound of traffic, but out here, in the trees, there is peace. Chirping birds. Scrabbling squirrels. A woodpecker high overhead. For the first time in ages her face feels clean.

With one hand, she pushes herself upright. Her other arm hurts — ah yes, it's in a sling. She had a fall; she tries to remember the details. She fell in the street and couldn't get up again, an ambulance came, took her to the hospital; they patched her up, told her off, and sent her on her way. That's right. Now she's here, in Stanley Park, under the trees, not far from the seawall where she used to cycle with Sarah and Frannie. Not far from Lion's Gate Bridge. Although Ireni doesn't have much of a sense of direction, she can always find her way to the bridge. She likes to be near the bridge, because of her Cousin Sasha. It's as though the bridge speaks to her, through the trees.

Maybe she'll get up and go down to the seawall; there will be joggers and cyclists and other early-morning people, the ladies who do power-walking. But it occurs to her that she has no idea of the time; here in the trees there is no direct sunlight. It could be morning, it could be midafternoon. She'll get up anyway. She looks around for her bag.

Her Pacific Tours bag. Brand new. In it, a bottle of gin, only two-thirds empty. More comes back to her now, in pieces; yesterday, on Robson Street — was it Robson? — she found the bag. Discarded by some cruise boat tourist, most likely, it was on the ground next to a garbage can — not in the garbage, mind you. Standards. She bent over to fetch it, and when she straightened up there was a woman standing right in front of her. Annie. Annie Bagshaw. The name sounded in her head, like an alarm bell. Ireni doesn't like running into people she knows; and people she knows don't like running into her. This one, Annie, covered her nose and mouth with her scarf, involuntarily, as though Ireni's very breath might be diseased. 'Ireni!' she shrieked, 'how are you?' She blushed at her own question.

'Oh very well, thank you,' Ireni replied. 'Very well indeed.'

Annie, at a loss, began fumbling with her purse. 'The girls are well.'

Ireni wasn't sure if this was a statement or a question. 'Which girls?'

'Mine.'

'Oh.'

'And yours?'

Ireni decided not to reply. She couldn't have begun to reply. She watched Annie fiddle with her purse. Annie had become a blonde since they last met. Ireni remembered having read somewhere that blonde was the best strategy when it came to covering grey. Well, it worked for Annie.

'Here,' said Annie, and she thrust a wad of money forward.

Ireni looked down at it, uncertain what to do. 'Take it.' Ireni did-n't move. Annie reached over and pulled open Ireni's coat pocket and stuffed the money inside. 'Have something nutritious to eat.'

Ireni looked up at her old acquaintance. On bridge club nights Ireni would often volunteer to be partnered with Annie for the first hand. At the time Annie appeared to think this meant they were great friends, but really Ireni just wanted to get it over and done with. Annie's determination to win made Ireni play really badly. Those long evenings of cards: salted peanuts and licorice all-sorts. Cocktails. There were a few things about her former life she missed.

'Actually, Ireni,' Annie snapped her purse shut and sighed. 'Why should we pretend? Buy yourself a drink. Put us all out of your misery.' And with that, she walked away.

Then the following sequence of events, Ireni thinks: fall, hos-pital, liquor store, and now here, Stanley Park. One thousand acres, the green lung, the tufty dark bit in the aerial photograph of the city that Tony has on the wall of his study; in summer Ireni used to bring Sarah and Frannie for rides on the toy train that ran near the zoo.

And now, in the forest, Ireni slips her hand into her pocket to see if there's any of Annie's money left. Much to her surprise, there is. Twenty dollars. She hauls herself up out of the leafy mulch in which she has slept, attempts a one-handed brush down and tidy up, tucks her hair behind her ears. Zips up her Pacific Tours bag. She will go find something nutritious to eat. And then she will have a drink. She will follow the edict laid down by Annie. Put herself out of her misery.

Christmas Eve. Vancouver. Pouring rain. Fran and Nick are there for the holiday. Everyone — Tony, Sarah, Nick, Fran — is studiously enjoying themselves. They've cooked a meal; they've wrapped the presents and decorated the tree; they are in the family room playing Monopoly. They've had the game for more than twenty years and pieces — houses, hotels, men, cards, players, money — are missing, rendering the game almost unplayable. Every time each of them notices a shortfall, they think of Ireni, as though it's her fault the game is a mess. But no one says a thing.

The trip to the lake had been a turning point. Summer before last. Before then Ireni had left home fairly often; since then, she left more and more frequently. At the slightest flare-up — Tony objecting to her drinking vodka at lunchtime, Sarah offering her a glass of water at supper when she had asked for more wine — she'd leave. She'd walk straight out the door without taking anything, not even her handbag, her wallet, her keys. At first, she'd be gone a week, then the absences got longer, and longer. Ten days. Two weeks. The length of time she was gone from the house surpassed the amount of time she was at home; she'd turn up for a bath, some food, clean clothes, money, and after three or four days, a week at most, she'd be gone again. There was nothing Tony or Sarah could do to stop her. She didn't want help. She just wanted to leave.

There's a rap on the front door. Tony peers through the curtains, but it's a black wet night and he can't see a thing. Moments later, they hear faint singing. Fran goes to the door and opens it, smiling, expecting carol-singers or the next-door neighbours bearing eggnog.

It's Ireni. She is naked, her skin streaked with blood and mud, stuck-on leaves, and rain. She has on one shoe, an oversized man's sandal, and a Tilley hat. She is drunk — of course — and she is shivering violently against the cold as she hums the tune to 'Silent Night'.

Before Fran can move forward to draw her mother to her, Tony pushes past, throws a blanket over his wife's head, and bundles her inside, like a suspect in a murder trial. Before anyone else can speak, he tells his daughters that he will deal with it, he will deal with their mother. They don't protest. He helps Ireni upstairs where he bathes her, dresses her in a matched set of her own clean pajamas that he had ironed and folded and put away after her last visit, and puts her into bed. He talks to her softly all the while: 'You're home now. You're home now, Ireni.'

Downstairs, Nick and Fran and Sarah sit around the Monopoly board, but they do not play. Nick counts his money. Fran and Sarah do nothing, say nothing. Neither daughter asks out loud what happened to their mother, where she could have been — what happened to her clothes, why she was bleeding, where the sandal and the hat came from. The unasked questions fill the room, the opposite of silence. Nick counts his money again. When the neighbours ring the bell, bearing eggnog, they do not answer.

Ireni sleeps through Christmas Day.

Days passed, time passed, and Fran and Leslie were still in Las Vegas. Back at Leslie's office, her staff were pissed off; Leslie could tell by the way her partner Karen said, 'You're still there? Oh, good for you Leslie.' They knew she hadn't taken a proper holiday in years, so they tried to keep their disapproval to themselves, Leslie heard them try, and fail. But Leslie hadn't felt so happy in ages. She was more suntanned than she'd ever been in her entire life. She'd played more blackjack than she would have thought possible. For the first time ever she'd gone way beyond her budget; she'd lost her original twenty grand, oh, what felt like weeks ago. She lost another ten grand. She stopped counting.

Fran and Leslie would talk in the middle of the night. Leslie would come in from the tables around 3 or 4 a.m. A little pissed, happy, satiated despite the fact that she was losing money. Fran would wake up when she came in and quiz her while she got ready for bed.

'Who'd you meet tonight?'

'Nobody.'

'Oh, come on.'

'Ebenezer — Kentucky.'

Fran giggled.

'Hepsibah — Montana.'

'Who else?'

'The usual gang. What have you been up to?'

'Studying for my PhD in casino administration.'

Leslie laughed, and then felt tired. She climbed into bed and turned out the light.

After a while Fran spoke up across the dark room. She had a way of asking the most piercing, pertinent questions when Leslie was half asleep. And somehow the dark, and the drink, and the cards she had consumed allowed Leslie to reply.

'Do you come here as a way of escaping what happened to Charlotte?'

For a moment Leslie felt disoriented. Was she really sharing a Vegas hotel room with a woman she hardly knew?

'I used to come to Las Vegas before Charlotte died,' she said. 'In those days I played blackjack for fun. Now I play because I have to, because nothing else holds any meaning.'

Another night Fran asked, 'What was it like when she died?'

'Oh Jesus,' Leslie said. 'You can't ask me that.'

Silence.

'It was — it was the worst time. I thought I would die with the pain of losing her. I wanted to die. I hoped to die. Death was too good for me.'

As always, when it came to talking about losing Charlotte, words failed Leslie and she found herself spouting guff. As though language on its own couldn't bear the weight of her grief. 'Death was too good for me,' she thought, what tripe. One day talking about losing Charlotte would render her wordless, the next day, full of bullshit. It wasn't possible to tell Fran — to tell anyone — what losing her was like.

The good thing for Leslie about these nighttime conversations was that Fran knew when to remain silent. She'd ask her question, and she'd listen to Leslie's reply. She'd never say, 'Oh you don't mean that!' She'd never say, 'I'm sorry, really, I'm so sorry,' or anything of the other well-meaning but useless things people say when confronted by loss. After Charlotte's death Leslie got to a point where she thought she would explode with rage if one more person told her they were sorry, told her they were so, so sorry. But then they stopped, they stopped saying it, they stopped asking about her baby and apologizing and suddenly it was as though Charlotte had never lived, let alone died, and so Leslie hated them for that as well.

But Fran knew better and she'd move the conversation onto something else. 'Why did you go into real estate? In London, estate agents are all complete shysters.'

'Shysters!' Leslie said. 'How can you speak of my brethren that way?'

'It's true! They'd gezump their sister. Anyway, why did you become a realtor?'

It was a kind of fluke, Leslie's choice of career. Her husband David finished his PhD and got his first real job; she could finally raise her head from the receptionist's desk and wonder if there was life beyond office work. They were living in a student rental out near the university, a one-bedroom apartment in a dilapidated building from the fifties — Formica counters with round corners and black and white linoleum. They decided it was time to buy a place of their own.

In the evenings, on the weekends, during her lunch break, Leslie began to look at houses. She met her first real estate agent, a woman called Janet Brushhead; all the lawyers she worked for used her and, at the time, she was one of the most successful agents in Vancouver. A power-dresser who favoured red suits — this was the 1980s — she was the most colossally ambitious person Leslie had ever met, ten times more ambitious than any of the lawyers she knew, so hugely ambitious that it was difficult to remember anything else about her, including what she looked like, as though the size of her drive obliterated everything else.

David used to say the source of her ambition was her name, Janet Brushhead; Leslie longed to ask if Brushhead was her married name, but she couldn't rely on herself to keep a straight face.

Janet could sell a house. She took on the many roles of the real estate agent — interior designer/cleaner/personal assistant/confessor/marriage counsellor — with a gusto that was humbling. And although Leslie knew she was a complete huckster, that the only reason she got up every day was in order to make the sale, she felt she could trust her. That was the key to her success. Everyone — vendor and vendee alike — trusted Janet Brushhead. She sold more houses per week than all the other agents in the city put together. In fact, sometimes Leslie liked to tell herself that Vancouver would still be a dirty old logging town, somewhere north of the US border, if Janet Brushhead hadn't sold so many houses.

Anyway, Janet inspired her. Janet made Leslie think, if she can do it, so can I. And Leslie had a good idea of her own, something she'd heard that people were starting to do in Toronto at the time: the property rollover. Buy an old house, do it up, sell it on. Make a profit. Buy two old houses, do them up, sell them on. Make an even bigger profit. Buy a really big old house, knock it down, subdivide, and build three new houses on the lot. And so on. Speculate.

Over the years Leslie acquired something of a reputation. Even though she started out doing renos, she liked new build, she liked to demolish. She had no qualms about razing to the ground what in Vancouver passes for 'heritage buildings'. Most of the houses the preservationists wanted to preserve were thrown up in the 1930s; they were badly built, and since then, they've weathered badly. Vancouver has an extraordinary climate:

temporate rainforest. In winter it rains continuously, day after day after day. That combined with the sea air; well, Leslie tells her clients, you can imagine what all of this moisture does to building materials. The whole leaky condo crisis — ordinary people left with worthless, dripping, mouldy, unsaleable properties all over the lower mainland — could have been avoided if only they'd listened to Leslie.

'Ha!' says Leslie to Fran. 'Who on earth would listen to me?'

She got out of the developer's game a while back, just before the crash in the nineties. 'I've gone back to basics,' she tells Fran, 'selling houses. It's what I do best, what I enjoy.' But, back then, egged on by Janet Brushhead, she had to find a way to get her foot in the door. She left the law firm where she'd worked for a couple of centuries, got a secretarial job in one of the city's top real estate firms, and started taking evening classes to get her licence. She watched. She waited. Then she made her first sale.

And her second sale. And her third.

Soon after that came the boomtime for the so-called 'tiger economies' — Hong Kong, Singapore, Taiwan, Korea. Vancouver, already aligned to these other Pacific Rim countries through immigration as well as commerce, was in a prime position to benefit, and benefit it did. 'To make a long story short,' says Leslie, 'so did I.'

'An East Indian friend of mine,' she continues, 'Sunetra, and I were having dinner together not long ago; she was telling me about a cousin of hers who was having difficulty securing his Canadian citizenship. "It would be very different, of course," she said, "if he were wealthy."

'"The thing is," I said to her — I had met with my accountant earlier that day — "once you've got money it's easy to make more. It's not exactly fair."

'My friend nodded. "*Maya ko maya milay, kar kar lambe haath*," she said. "It's a Hindi saying. It means—" she waved her hand, "wealth greets wealth with outstretched hand. Or better, money finds money."

'"Money is waiting for money with open arms?"

'"You've got it." She smiled.

'And it was true,' Leslie said to Fran. 'As soon as I'd banked my first hundred grand, I had it made.'

Much to Leslie's surprise, making money did not automatically make life easier. It turned out that David was neither enamoured of her success, nor her choice of career. It wasn't a breadwinner thing, and it wasn't jealousy; as far as men go, he wasn't particularly bound by traditional roles. He had a scientist's distain for business, despite the fact that his employer was owned by one of the world's largest mining companies. But Leslie thinks their problem, even then, was more profound than that. 'The fact is,' Leslie tells Fran, 'geologists are weird and field geologists are even weirder. David liked rocks more than people. David liked rocks more than me.'

But it wasn't until after Charlotte died that this became apparent.

So Fran and Leslie talked, night after night. Truth be told, Fran didn't say much about herself. Leslie thought it was like living with an amnesiac. The beautiful brunette gets hit on the head and can no longer remember her own name. Leslie wondered if Fran had some kind of post-natal depression, but she wasn't sure, and there was something else as well, other factors that had driven her away from her home, her child.

Once, late at night, Leslie decided it was her turn to ask the questions. 'Why did you leave London?' she said.

Silence. Leslie thought she wasn't going to answer. But, after a moment, Fran cleared her throat and spoke. 'Would you split a pair of eights?'

'Jesus H. Christ, Fran, how can you have been in this city, in this hotel, for all this time and not know the answer to that? It depends entirely on what the dealer is showing.' Leslie embarked on a lengthy explanation, completely forgetting her own question. She had, after all, been drinking. In the morning, in the shower, the conversation came back to her. But by then it was too late.

The following night Fran spoke first. 'I loved working,' she said. 'I'm a rubbish mother.'

Oh, that's not true, Leslie almost said, but then she stopped herself. Maybe it was true. Who was she to say? After all, Fran had run away; what could be more — as Fran would say — rubbish than that?

Leslie tried a different angle. 'What about your own mother?'

'What about her?'

'Well, what kind of mother was she?'

'She was a rubbish mother as well,' Fran laughed.

'Was she?'

'She drank. Drinks.'

'You told me that.'

'Yes.' Fran took a deep breath and sighed as though she'd told this story a million times, when, in fact, she'd never talked about it before. She couldn't talk about it, she'd never been able to tell any of her friends, not even Claire. Claire knew about the drinking and the disappearing, but she had no idea how far it had gone. It was too terrible, too painful, to make it part of ordinary day-to-day conversation. 'She lives on the street.'

Leslie was glad the room was dark so that Fran didn't have to see her face. 'She does?'

'Yes.'

'Where?' For a moment Leslie pictured an older version of Fran wandering up and down Las Vegas Boulevard, endlessly.

'Vancouver.'

'How did that happen?'

'She drank. She drinks.'

'Yes, but—'

'It happens. Middle-class woman gone astray.'

'But Fran, it's an extreme—'

'I know.'

They lay in the dark, Fran in her bed, Leslie in hers, contemplating Fran's words. How could it happen? How could Fran's mother end up on the street?

She spoke up again. 'She had a job once, for a while, when I was about ten, I think.'

'What was it?'

'Cocktail waitress.'

'No.' It was hard not to laugh.

'Yes.' Fran giggled.

'Did she last long?'

'No.'

'No,' Leslie replied.

'Anyway,' Fran said, 'it's hard to talk about it.'

Leslie pulled the covers up around her chin; she'd turned the air-con up too high when she came in the room. She thought she couldn't begin to understand what Fran had just told her; it was too late, she was too tired, it was too huge a thing.

Fran left her baby while Leslie's had been taken away from her; it wasn't right, and it wasn't fair. Leslie knew she should have been jumping up and down, outraged. But she wasn't.

Fran stopped working because she had a child. She stopped working, and she went crazy. Leslie understood that completely.

Fran's mother was a street person. Call me too-quick-to-jump-to-easy-conclusions, Leslie thought, but that explains a lot about my roommate to me.

In the dark Leslie heard Fran turn over onto her side; the beds in the room were very comfortable, neatly made, the sheets clean and crisp, the blankets heavy and soft. Leslie settled down to sleep. Would she dream about Charlotte? Most likely.

At night, alone in bed, this is what Leslie sees: her big old house. It's a sunny day.

She steps into the sitting room. She looks up. She sees Charlotte. She's in the air. For a moment Leslie thinks she can fly. My baby can fly! But it's not true. Now she understands. Her baby.

She wakes up. Except that's not true either, she doesn't ever wake up. Because it's not a dream.

'Tell me again, Fran: why did you decide to come to Las Vegas? Couldn't you have gone somewhere a little more… local? I don't know— Bournemouth? Brighton?'

'Well,' Fran said, 'I got on the tube and I went to the airport. I had a choice between Las Vegas, Tehran, Tel Aviv, and Kigali. So I chose Las Vegas.' She laughed. 'It made sense to me at the time.'

A little while later, Fran asked her question; sometimes conversation seemed to Leslie like little more than elaborate sparring, an I for an I — I'll tell you this if you tell me that.

'Why did your marriage fail?' Fran asked.

'Our baby died.'

'Yes, but that might have brought you closer together.'

'We'd stopped talking to each other years before that. I tried, but he didn't want to talk. You can't make people talk.'

'No,' said Fran, 'you cannot.'

'You know,' Leslie said, 'a friend of mine once said to me that it had taken her a long time to realize that her husband couldn't be her friend. That he was a good husband, and a good father, and a good man, but he wasn't going to talk to her. But, she said, she'd decided that it didn't matter. At the time — we were both still pretty young — what she said horrified me. Who'd want to live with a man you couldn't talk to? And then, over the years, David got quieter and quieter, and more and more reluctant to say anything much at all to me. And I thought, well, that's okay. He loves me and I love him, and Charlotte, well, once she learned to speak, she talked all the time.'

'So it worked, in its way?'

'I had friends I could talk to.'

They lay in the dark silence for a while, bound together by their late-night confessional.

'But then, when we needed to talk to each other, we couldn't. We'd forgotten how. And what's more, it became apparent that we had both moved on so far, both changed so much, we were different people. The man I married and the man I divorced were not the same person.'

Fran didn't say anything. So, after a while, Leslie spoke up again. 'Have you left your husband, Fran?'

She didn't reply.

One day Leslie hired a car. 'I do not want to go look at those damned red rocks,' she said; she had her feet up on the dash, Fran was driving. 'My ex-husband — what was his name? — he took me there.'

'I'd like to see Red Rock Canyon,' said Fran.

'I would never have taken you for a geology major.'

'My dad's a rock guy.'

'He is? You never told me that.'

'He's a paleontologist.'

'Dinosaurs.'

'No. Tiny fossils. Tiny fossils that, he says, hold the secret of the universe inside. Anyway, I'd just like to see the red rocks, okay?'

Despite the depth and breadth of the concept, Vegas peters out pretty quickly and then you are out in the desert. Desert hills in the distance, and a flat, broken tin-can tumbleweed plain all around. Not a nice desert, Leslie thought, not a picturesque Roadrunner/Coyote/Grand Canyon kind of place. Dirt. And heat.

They missed the turn-off for the park somehow and ended up in Pahrump. Prostitution is legal in a number of counties in Nevada, although not in Clark County, which is where Vegas is, and Pahrump, rather famously, has the brothels closest to the city, carefully patrolled and regulated by the local authority. As they drove through, it looked like any other low-rent dustbowl town. Peeling billboards advertising 'Terrible's Slots' and 'Terrible's Ham and Eggs' ('Seems there's a casino called Terrible's out this way,' said Leslie), a drive-in fast-food place, at least a dozen evangelical churches, a half-closed strip mall flying an enormous US flag, and any number of dead-end streets.

'If I were a hooker,' Leslie said, 'I would not want to live in this place.'

'Well,' said Fran, 'it looks kind of peaceful to me. You've got your mall, your church, your casino, your house of ill-repute — what more could you need?'

After Pahrump they continued to drive for what felt like hours but was probably more like twenty minutes. The highway stretched out into the desert. They rounded an enormous curve in the road and began to travel downhill toward what looked like a vast inland sea. No water, no vegetation. High grey mountains ringing it; in the middle a series of sudden black hills, like mining slag heaps, except there'd never been any industry here.

Behind the black hills, as though hidden away from prying eyes, a small scrappy oasis, birch trees glinting. This was Crystal. 'Mabel's House of Prostitution', 'Madam Butterfly's', and 'The Cherry Patch Ranch' all turned out to be more or less the same place. The rest of the town consisted of a collection of bungalows with screen doors with holes in them and mobile homes that were drifting away from their foundations.

Fran pulled the car off the road and into the empty parking lot of a place called 'Big Juicy's'. The brothel buildings were low-rise, tacked together. Leslie noticed that near the front door there was a handicapped parking space. Nice. A homemade sign read, 'Welcome to Big Juicy's' and 'Please Ring the BELL for Service' in smaller lettering below. The curtains on the windows were drawn tight. It looked as though no one had visited for quite some time. Since 1965 maybe, thought Leslie.

'Why would anyone drive all the way out here when they can have a naked girl in their room in twenty minutes back at Caesars?' Leslie asked. She'd picked a leaflet up off the sidewalk just the other day.

'It's legal,' said Fran.

They sat and stared at 'Big Juicy's'. There should have been a screen door flapping on rusty hinges and a mangy half-wild dog barking out back. But instead there was an unearthly silence. Leslie felt sure the town was below sea level; the atmosphere felt unnaturally heavy. If she got out of the car she'd be unable to lift her limbs due to the extra force of gravity.

'Should we go in?' asked Fran.

Leslie shook her head. 'I doubt we'd be welcome. It's not a zoo. There's real girls in there, trying to make a living.' She felt a bit sick.

'How much do they make?' asked Fran. 'In a month, for instance?'

'Oh Jesus Fran, don't even ask. How would I know anyway?'

'It's an honest living.'

'Oh please. "All women are prostitutes. The smart ones get paid." Are you considering a career change?'

'All women are housewives,' said Fran. She looked at Leslie. 'I need a plan.'

Leslie had had enough. 'Look honey, you need a plan, I'll buy you a plan. Just don't include the town of Crystal in it, whatever you are thinking. Take me home,' she said. 'Return to Caesar.'

But Fran wasn't listening. She was looking at Big Juicy's. There was no other movement, no sign of any occupants. Leslie tried to roll down the window but the engine was turned off, so she opened the car door to let in the breeze. There was no breeze, only the sound of the earth baking, like a garden hose hissing, though she knew no one had watered anything around here for a long time.

After a while, they turned around, and drove back to Las Vegas.

That night when Leslie got back to the room after her stint at the tables, Fran was asleep. Or, at least, she appeared to be. Leslie was surprised to feel a little pang of disappointment. She had a hot bath — her shoulders ached with tension, for a while she'd been rather lucky that evening — climbed into bed and fell asleep.

Leslie woke a couple of hours later. It was 4 a.m. Fran's bed was empty.

She got up. Fran wasn't in the bathroom. Her linen dress was gone. Leslie had bought her a couple of items of clothing, a summer dress, a pair of pants, a couple of t-shirts, some underwear, and a bathing suit; Fran hadn't asked for anything, but Leslie went ahead and did it anyway. Everything was in Fran's drawer, neatly folded. She'd taken her handbag. She'd made her bed. Leslie found herself wondering if Fran really existed. Maybe I've lost my mind and Fran is the other half of my split personality.

Leslie got dressed and went out into the hotel corridor, down in the elevator. She wandered around the casino floor for a while; it was relatively quiet and if Fran had been there, Leslie would have found her. She completed her circuit and stopped at the front entrance to the casino. She peered through the dark glass; outside the valets were ready to park and fetch, as always. She looked around the foyer, unsure whether she should head out, away from the hermetically sealed World of Caesar. She took a deep breath and pushed through the revolving door.

Outside, she was hit with a blast of heat. Hot at night, Leslie loved a city that was hot at night. The sky was a deep purple, with only a whispered suggestion that soon it would get light. 'Did you see a woman leave,' she asked the doorman, sweaty in his uniform, 'pale skin, long hair, handbag?'

The doorman pushed out his lower lip in thought. 'In a car?'

'I'm not sure. White linen dress. Pale.'

He shook his head. She figured if he'd flagged a taxi for her, he'd remember. She must have gone on foot.

Leslie decided to walk toward the Mirage. Maybe Fran suddenly had an urge to go watch the volcano erupt. Or see the white tigers. Or watch the sharks swim round in their tank. Or maybe she went over to the Bellagio to see the fountains dance to Sinatra tunes. Leslie liked to think people come to Vegas to gamble but, these days, she's wrong.

Vegas is not meant for walkers. Even the efforts the casinos have made toward encouraging foot traffic — pedestrian bridges, moving sidewalks, long gently sloping escalators complete with soundtracks and light-shows — don't encourage walking as such, but more straightforward conveyance from one casino to the next. Las Vegas Boulevard — the Strip — stretches on forever; the casinos are huge and surrounded by vast areas of landscaping.

Walking from one casino to the next requires great determination. Leslie decided that if she set a brisk pace, chance was she'd catch up with Fran sooner or later.

Late at night it is possible to catch glimpses of what Vegas was once like. Late at night the new-fangled Disneyfied mask slips a little, enough for people like Leslie — those who are looking — to see the disfigured face beneath. Vice, as American TV cops like to call it: very young prostitutes, not so young drug dealers, the homeless, the lost, the abandoned, the people the city likes to pretend don't exist. And somewhere out there, Fran, wandering. She'd said she needed a plan. Now Leslie was worried.

After a while, she gave up. She'd been walking for what felt like ages, but the Mirage looked even farther away. She was not going to find her, out there in the Vegas night. She headed back to Caesars, toward the main entrance.

And there Fran was, standing in front of the revolving door. Maybe she'd been inside the casino all this time. In the night heat and neon Fran's white linen dress shimmered and blinked, like a malfunctioning computer screen. She turned toward Leslie, waving.

Fran and Leslie had been at Caesars Palace for nine days. Nine days! Leslie had never stayed so long in Vegas. Even she could admit it wasn't healthy.

The next morning, Leslie got both herself and Fran on a plane to Vancouver. Fran objected — she owed Leslie enough money already. 'I can't just leave you here,' Leslie said. 'The next occupant of that room might not be as sweet-natured as me.' Leslie hadn't set out to be charitable to Fran, or kind, or even particularly friendly. But when Fran happened, Leslie said to herself, she happened to me.

CONFINEMENT

She had planned to have the baby at home. With hindsight, she can't think what possessed her, what made her think it would be okay. She and Nick hired a birth pool from the Active Birth Centre up in Archway. Fran imagined that she'd slip in and out of it like a big sleek mermaid. It arrived the week the baby was due and they assembled it together; it was large and blue and smelled of new plastic. When Celine dropped round she was horrified. 'If I had to do it, I'd want a general anesthetic and a Caesarian and a night nanny and a wet nurse.' Fran and Nick smiled at her benevolently.

Fran went into labour on Saturday evening, four days after the baby was due. It started off very calmly. The contractions — every fifteen minutes or so — felt like stops and starts on a Ferris wheel, little earth tremors; she needed to grab onto something in order to maintain her balance, even when she was sitting. 'Probably pre-labour,' the midwife said on the phone. Despite all the classes and books, Fran had never heard of pre-labour. You think it's labour, it hurts like labour, but really, it's just your body practising. 'Pre-labour' was the first indication to Fran that things were not going to go according to plan — not according to the birth plan she'd drawn up, not according to anyone's plan.

Nick got busy, filling the huge blue plastic birth pool with warm water.

During the night, the pains increased in pressure and duration and began to come closer together. She tried to time them, clutching her clock and counting: every four or five minutes. They crept up on her, overwhelmed her, ravaged her, and then slid away. Again. And again. Nick slept for a while, but he didn't want to leave Fran by herself. He wandered back and forth — sitting room, bedroom, sitting room, bedroom — and back and forth again.

The midwife came round in the morning and listened to the baby's heart and said everything was fine.

'Isn't the baby coming now?' Fran asked.

The midwife smiled. 'You're fine. You've got a way to go yet. You're fine.'

Fran, trying not to despair, asked if she could get into the pool.

The water felt glorious. It was warm and soft and the buoyancy helped support the tremendous weight that Fran was carrying. She relaxed immediately. The room was dark, the curtains shut tight against the day. Nick put some music on and she stretched her arms along the rim and let her body float. Lamplight reflected off the water and rippled bluely across the ceiling. Fran closed her eyes. The pain began to slip away. The contractions got slower and slower, and further and further apart, until they were back to every fifteen minutes or so.

Fran stayed in the pool until she was white and wrinkled. Then she got out, draped herself in clean towels, and helped Nick with the pool cover. In midafternoon the midwife phoned again. 'Try to get some rest,' she said. Nick went into the bedroom, fell on the bed, and was asleep. Fran curled up on the settee. She'd dose off, and then a contraction would wake her. She'd dose off, and it would happen again. Every fifteen minutes. She could hear Nick snoring.

The midwife phoned in the early evening. 'Go for a walk,' she said, 'let's get this baby moving.'

So they went for a walk, past the shops and the cafés and the gallery. Every couple of minutes they'd run into someone they knew. While they chatted, Fran would lean against the nearest parked car, the closest lamppost. 'Are you okay?' their friends would ask. 'Oh,' Nick waved his hand, 'don't worry. She's only in labour.' Everyone laughed heartily. Then they'd look at Fran, her knuckles white, her teeth clenched, and say 'Oh my god, she is, isn't she?'

Eventually, after this conversation had been repeated several times, Fran hissed at Nick, 'If we don't go home now I'm going to squat down right here and never get up again.'

The pool came with instructions that said it had to be emptied every twenty-four hours to stop infectious bacteria developing. That evening, Sunday, Nick ran a hose through to the bathtub and tried to get some suction going. He ended up bailing most of the water into the kitchen sink. It took him an hour. The floor got wet and slippery, and then he filled the pool again.

That evening, the contractions sped up once more. Ten minutes, eight minutes, five minutes, four. Fran tried to keep moving, pacing the flat. It was much more painful now than it had been previously. Each contraction rolled in deep through her back, like a great steel shutter crashing down and then rising up again. The muscles inside her abdomen pulled and her enormous belly hardened like concrete. It went on and on, on through the night. She panted, she breathed, she walked, she squatted, she got down on her hands and knees. Nick rubbed her back, rubbed her shoulders, rubbed her feet. When the contractions were coming at three-minute intervals he rang the midwife. She arrived in fifteen minutes; it was 4 a.m. She examined Fran internally, as gently as she could, but still, Fran couldn't help but scream with pain. She'd never before heard herself scream with pain.

'Looking good,' the midwife announced. 'Five centimetres, thinning out nicely. You're doing well.'

'Only five?' Fran couldn't remember when she'd last felt so disappointed. Only halfway; five more centimetres to go. And why, Fran thought, is it always ten centimetres? Maybe her cervix was different, maybe hers was eleven. Fifteen.

'Five's good,' said the midwife, ever cheery. 'First babies sometimes take their time.'

'Can I get in the pool again?'

'Good idea. That will give you some relief.' She turned to Nick. 'Let me know how it's going.'

'You're not staying?'

'She's fine. The baby is happy. I'll come back in a few hours. Phone me if you have any worries.'

Jesus Christ, Nick thought, don't leave.

Once again, getting into the pool brought immediate relief. The warm weight of the water against her skin was soothing. But after a short time spent watching her bump break the surface of the water like a great round submarine, Fran realized the contractions were slowing down again. 'Nick,' she shrieked. He came running. 'I don't fucking want it to slow down.'

'Get out,' he shouted, 'get out of the water.'

She scrambled out of the pool, sloshing water down over the sides. 'Oh Jesus, oh Jesus,' she said. Nick threw piles of towels on the floor. Fran began to cry. The contractions had slowed down, and they were still slowing. Slowing. Slowing. Ten minutes. Eleven minutes. Right back down to fifteen.

Why did no one, Fran thought on Monday evening as the contractions began to pick up speed once again, why did no one fucking tell me? That the thing about labour, the thing about giving birth, is that it is absolutely beyond our control. You can do any amount of preparation but, in the end, it will take you by surprise, like an unexpected bombing campaign. And nobody tells you about the pain. Why did no one tell me about the pain?

The baby was fine. The midwife had returned with her sonic listening device; the baby's heart was beating steadily; the midwife left again. Fran wondered what it was like in there — was the baby adrift on a stormy sea, booming thunder, lashing waves, or was it warm and snug, given a firm-handed and oily massage by the contractions, but otherwise half-asleep and dreamy?

Nick emptied and refilled the pool once again.

Now it was Tuesday — 'It is now Tuesday,' Nick said out loud, although no one was listening, 'we began on Saturday' — and the sun was shining and life was going on outside the windows of their flat. Inside, the midwife had Fran on the bed. They had decided she would rupture the membranes in an attempt to get things moving. The bed was thick with towels and incontinence pads. The midwife was wielding an instrument that closely resembled a crotchet hook.

'When I was twelve I learned to crotchet,' Fran said. 'I might still have a spare hook somewhere.'

Nick laughed.

The midwife was concentrating.

'In Vancouver,' Fran added, 'in the basement.'

The midwife waited for the right moment between contractions and, in a single, practiced maneuver, stuck the hook up inside Fran, pushed it through her cervix, jammed it into the sac that contained volumes of amniotic fluid, the placenta, and the baby, and attempted to puncture it, to tear a small hole for the waters to break through. Fran did her best not to scream. Neither she, nor the procedure, was successful.

Because of the intervention with the crotchet hook, the risk of infection had increased exponentially. The midwife made Nick and Fran a cup of tea. 'We will have to go to hospital,' she said, grimly.

To hospital. For Fran, this felt like a tremendous defeat. Like a retreat from the front line, the battle lost. Her own body had betrayed her. You thought this was natural, it was saying, you thought this would be easy. Well, you're wrong, you got it all wrong, baby.

'I don't want to go to hospital.' Fran started to cry.

'Oh honey, we've got to go, this is—' Nick stopped.

'What?' said Fran, tearful and snotty and huge.

'This is ridiculous. God knows how much longer this might go on. And you can't—'

The midwife interrupted. 'Do you want to get this baby out?'

'Yes,' Fran wailed.

'It's time to go, love. Let's go to hospital.' She rubbed Fran's back. Fran cried.

Nick collected things to take. Going to hospital had not been in Fran's birth plan; he had no idea what they might need. He packed a vase, a large box of the raisins Fran had craved throughout her pregnancy, and a pillow.

Out on the street, they hailed a taxi and tumbled out at the front door of St Mary's as a double-decker bus bore down on them from behind, honking. In the delivery room torn curtains hung from the single filthy painted-shut window, a column of black soot rose above the ventilation shaft. The midwife busied herself with charts and consultations, speaking in a low voice outside in the corridor, flitting in and out of the room. Nick and Fran sat on the bed; they held hands. 'Oh boy,' Nick said, looking around. 'Here we are.'

The contractions had stopped almost entirely, as though they didn't want to be in hospital either. Fran thought maybe it just wasn't going to happen, she would have to stay nine months pregnant, six centimetres dilated, for the rest of her life.

'You should get something to eat,' she said to Nick, furious that she wasn't allowed anything herself now.

'Yeah,' said Nick. 'I'm starving.'

'Ask the midwife if she wants something.'

'Yeah,' he said, 'okay.' He got up and shuffled out of the room like a geriatric outpatient.

The midwife bustled in.

'A gown?' said Fran as the midwife helped ease her into the hospital garment. 'This is not a gown by my reckoning.'

And then— nothing. The fetal heart monitor to which Fran was now attached worked only sporadically, but when it did, it showed the baby was fine. The contractions returned, had a look round, and went away again. Eventually, a doctor arrived to examine Fran. 'Okay,' he said, 'let's get things moving.' Fran turned her head away.

More waiting. Fran could hear, down the corridor, a woman screaming. The anesthetist arrived and he gave Fran an epidural; she had to hold herself very still while he stuck a large needle into the base of her spine. And the midwife and the doctor set up a syntocinon drip. If Fran's body would not progress through labour on its own, medical science would do it for her. Soon Fran no longer had any sensation below her waist; she could be having the largest contraction in the history of womankind and she wouldn't have felt a thing. She was too tired and disappointed to feel relieved. She spoke to Nick, who was eating a sandwich. 'I wanted to feel it. I wanted to feel my baby.' Her voice was slurry.

'I know,' murmured Nick, 'I know.' No I don't, thought Nick, I know nothing.

And though it was the middle of the afternoon, the midwife dimmed the lights in the dingy room and Fran and Nick both fell into a waking sleep, half-aware of their surroundings, Fran propped up on the hospital bed, Nick slumped in the beige vinyl armchair with bits of stuffing hanging out on one side. It was quiet. The fetal heart monitor, strapped low around Fran's belly, came on and beeped reassuringly before malfunctioning again.

Some hours passed. Now it was close to midnight. The midwife roused Fran for an examination.

'You're fully dilated.'

'Hurray,' Fran said dully. 'Ten centimetres.' She lay down on her side and thought she might go to sleep again. But suddenly the room was full of people.

This was what it was like: the room dark apart from one enormous hot spotlight, teetering on its stand. People, lots and lots of people, other midwives, doctors, nurses, interns crowded into the room; for so long, for days and days, it had been just

Fran, Nick, and the midwife. Now everyone had arrived, and they looked like they'd be staying. The doctor, in his hospital greens, wheeled in a hooverish Heath Robinson contraption, the *ventouse*, the vacuum-suction machine; he pulled on his latex gloves and asked the nurse for the scalpel.

And Nick, poor Nick, was not prepared for this turn of events. Fran had read all the books, but he had not. He hadn't wanted to come to hospital either; he liked the idea of being at home. He didn't know what an epidural was; he had never heard of syntocinon and episiotomies and all those other ghastly, slippery-slope medical interventions: once you've had one, Fran said, you might as well have them all. So when the bed she'd been sitting on for hours and hours was suddenly stripped of its cover, when the bottom half swung down and the stirrups and leg braces came up and Fran's legs were strapped in, the fight went out of Nick and he slumped down into the battered armchair, and that was it for him, he thought they were goners, Fran and the baby.

Throughout the procedure the doctor kept one plastic-shod foot on the floor, the other braced against the end of the bed. This, Nick realized after a while, enabled him to gain better purchase, to have greater leverage, on the crown of the head of the baby he was attempting to suck or, indeed, *hoover*, out of Fran. Nick became convinced the doctor was yanking so hard, pulling with such tremendous force and tenacity, that he was going to rip the head off the baby.

And Fran, poor Fran, for her it was like one of those alien abduction stories she had heard people tell on daytime TV, so surreal, the pulsing spotlight, the dull roar of the *ventouse* machine, the people who when they weren't shouting commands were whispering sinisterly, and she was stuck there, in her great heaving, incapable body, strapped onto the medieval torture bed while tiny creatures ferreted away *down below.* Snip, snip, snip!

And, eventually, after what felt like hours and hours and days and days of roaring and pulling and yanking and sucking, the baby's head popped out of her body.

The doctor turned off the machine.

All was quiet.

'There you go,' said the midwife, and she helped Fran lean forward to see and it was as though Fran's own head was miles and miles away from that space between her legs, and down there, way, way, far away, there was indeed the head of a baby, dark, hair matted with fluid, turning to one side like an animated puppet in a macabre Eastern European animation. And Nick took a look as well, and he saw the head and in that moment suddenly remembered that, yes, they were having a baby, an actual baby, not some kind of terrifying medical nightmare. A few more minutes and Fran's body gave another great involuntary squeeze and the baby slid out into the doctor's waiting hands.

'A boy,' he said.

'A boy,' Nick said to Fran.

'A boy,' Fran said to herself.

Then the baby was whisked and frisked and dabbed and jabbed and wrapped and handed to Fran. She gazed down at him, carefully.

It was 2 a.m, Wednesday.

And six weeks later Fran was sitting in the bath, leaking milk from her cracked and bleeding nipples, her episiotomy stitches failing to heal, her lower back still haunted by a dull post-epidural ache, the baby waking and fretful in the next room, having been asleep for no longer than fifteen minutes at a stretch all day, her stomach a large flap of loose skin despite the painful downsizing contractions of her uterus, on her own most days, in alone most evenings: Fran found herself thinking, when's it going to end? When is it going to stop hurting? Where's my mum? Where's Ireni?

BC

Ireni woke up longing to be in the water. Although it was early, it was already hot. She had thrown off her sheet and her nightie was stuck to her back. There was a small hole in the screen where her little brother had poked his pencil; the bedroom was already full of flies, circling the ceiling, scrabbling at the window in an effort to get away. They buzzed; John snored. She got up, pulled on her bathing suit and shorts, and went to wake up Sasha.

Sasha got to sleep in the outside porch with Ireni's big brothers. It wasn't fair. He was the same age as her, seven. Before, he'd slept in her room. But when he came to stay this summer he got to sleep outside.

There was a place on the river, beyond the gas station on the highway, where the stream widened and the current slowed. The gravel banks had allowed a shallow lagoon to form and here the water was clear and still, warmed by the sun, not the usual surging milky green of the river as it charged by. By the end of the morning the swimming hole would be full of children, but Ireni and Sasha got there before anyone else every day.

Sasha was a boy but Ireni didn't mind; they were cousins. Their families used to live together in the big house on the farm. That was a long time ago, before John was born, before Ireni's parents moved into town and got their own house and her father went to work in the sawmill. Sasha's parents stayed with Baba and

Grandpa in the big house. Ireni's papa said it was better that way, because Baba and Grandpa and Uncle and Auntie didn't believe in the Government's Laws. Ireni's papa said he was fed up, he was fed up with all of them at the farm.

No one was allowed to speak Russian anymore in Ireni's house, not even her mother, so the grown-ups all spoke bad English and were always confusing each other. That summer, after three years in elementary school, Ireni realized she could not remember any Russian words. This wasn't quite true; she could understand the grown-ups when their kitchen-table arguments grew loud in the night; at least, she could understand the words they used, if not what they actually meant. But her own lips could no longer form the proper word-shapes and the sounds that emerged were baby-ish, not right.

'Speak it,' she commanded Sasha as they took turns on the rope swing. Already — school had only finished a week ago — she had rope burns on her hands and inside her thighs. Another week and they would turn into callouses. Sasha didn't go to school; his parents were teaching him at home on the farm. It wasn't fair. When she asked her mama about it, she said Sasha's parents were too stubborn and that it was dangerous and that even though the Government had said he had to go to school, he did not. Ireni felt envious of her cousin's freedom but Sasha did-n't speak English very well, so she figured that made them even.

Sasha grabbed the swing away from her and flew out over the water, shouting in his big Russian voice, 'We are Doukhobor! The Sons of Freedom! The True Spirit Wrestlers! And all that bullshit!' — the last part in English. As he came back toward her she could tell he wasn't going to let go of the rope so she grabbed him round his waist, and they swung together out over the water, the extra weight bringing them both down with a great splash.

Ireni remembered the farm, although her parents did not take her there anymore, and she remembered the house, and she remembered when it felt like they had been there forever, in the orchard, and they would be there forevermore. They'd had more land once, but it had been taken away by the Government a long time ago. The families grew cherries and peaches on what was left and, in summer, the children's hands and faces were always sticky and stained with juice. Ireni never saw her grandparents now; it was as though her own parents were afraid of them, although she could not — try as she might — figure out why.

'You are Canadian girl,' her mother was always saying. 'We assimilate,' pronounced slowly and carefully. For a long time Ireni thought 'assimilate' was another word for Canadian and, later, she realized she wasn't that far from the truth.

Her parents were determined to leave the old ways behind; this was one of the things that they argued about with Sasha's parents in the night. 'It's crazy!' Ireni heard her mama saying. 'They'll think it was you. They'll blame you.'

'We have our own Laws,' Uncle said in his sternest voice, 'the Laws of Christ.'

'You'll protest against anything,' her father replied. 'It's not right,' he continued, 'it's not — modern,' this last word almost whispered, as though it was secret code for the good life.

Whenever the grown-ups were together these days, they argued. Up north, the Sons of Freedom had taken to more extreme measures, including arson attacks, which Ireni knew meant burning things, setting fires. Schools, Government buildings, even houses; she heard Uncle talking about a man he knew who had burnt down the house of the local Mountie. Her parents were horrified; this was not the way they wanted to live their lives. 'We've moved into town,' she heard her father insisting, 'we've moved into town and we live like Canadians. We are not Sons of Freedom, we are not Doukhobor — we are Canadian.' When he said this, Ireni's mama began to cry.

There were other Doukhobor children in the town, and Ireni saw that they were allowed to be both Doukhobor and Canadian. Their families had no connection with the Freedomites up the road. Like Ireni, they wore Canadian clothes to school, but, unlike Ireni, they were allowed to wear traditional clothes on special occasions. And they spoke Russian to each other freely when they gathered in their meeting place. They were ordinary. Ireni watched them; she knew their names. She knew their parents weren't afraid. She wished her family could be like them.

Earlier that year Uncle had been arrested, yet again, for using pink farmer's gasoline in his car. The farm gas was much cheaper than the regular. 'I'm a farmer. I can't see why I shouldn't put it in my car,' was all he had to say on the matter.

Ireni went to the courthouse in Nelson with her parents. On the way she sat in the middle of the back seat; she'd fought with both John and Sasha over the window seats and lost. They'd risen in the dark in order to arrive on time, fetching Auntie on the way; both Uncle and his car were in custody. On the journey Auntie was, as always, polite and serene; she smelt of bread making. But when her husband emerged from the cells, and the charges were read out, Ireni could feel her aunt's increasing agitation. She was fiddling with her clothes, undoing buttons, fidgeting. No one, apart from Ireni, took any notice until, moments later, Auntie stood up. There she was, in the courtroom, naked.

She was skinny and baggy at the same time, blue-veined and goose-bumped in the winter morning, but it was her breasts that were, to Ireni, extraordinary. There they were. Auntie's boobies. The police carried her away, shouting.

That was it as far as Ireni's parents were concerned, 'The last haystack,' her mother kept repeating. Auntie was fined for contempt of court and Uncle was fined a larger sum for using farm gasoline. From then on Ireni's parents saw even less of Sasha's. But Ireni didn't mind because her cousin was still allowed to come to stay; 'We can't punish the child for his parents' beliefs,' Ireni heard her father say.

And Sasha and Ireni ignored the grown-ups and their arguments, pushing their rope out over the water once again.

Fran stared out the window at the sea. The cloudbank had been solid all the way up the coast; it broke briefly over what might have been Puget Sound and Seattle, but then thickened up again, like porridge, tall and lumpy. As they began to descend through the grey she wished she could see the city, in order to be reminded of where she was heading. Leslie was asleep — she'd slept all the way from Vegas. She'd taken a pill when they got on the plane. Whereas Fran, over the past twenty-four hours, had been feeling more and more awake. More awake than she'd been for days, months — nearly two years: more awake than since she'd had Louis.

And now, whoosh, the plane was out of the clouds and over the water. Vancouver is wedged between the mountains and the sea; the airport sits right on the edge, on reclaimed river delta land. They touched down and the clouds were so low Fran hadn't even glimpsed the city.

Once through customs, Leslie stopped at the carousel to wait for her suitcase. Fran carried the few things Leslie had bought her in a Caesars Palace shopping bag. She could go through to the exit now; she'd find a telephone and ring her sister, Sarah, or perhaps her father, Tony; see if one of them could come out and fetch her.

She stopped beside Leslie, who wasn't yet fully awake.

'Good flight,' said Leslie.

'Do you always take a pill?'

Leslie nodded.

Fran opened her handbag and took out a piece of paper — Caesars hotel stationery. 'This is what I owe you.' She offered the long columns of figures.

Fran had included everything, itemized, from the ticket to Vancouver to the muffin she'd had for breakfast that morning. At the bottom she had drawn a box around the total. It was a shopkeeper's receipt. Leslie stared at it.

'Have I left something out?'

'Um,' said Leslie, 'not as far as I can see.' She ran her hand over her face and blinked hard, trying to wake up.

'Give me your address. I'll send you a cheque.'

The two women looked at each other.

'Or it might be a postal order. I don't know. Pounds sterling. This is US dollars. I'll figure it out.' Fran laughed. 'I'll use a calculator.'

They stood in silence. The baggage carousel went round and round. Neither could think what to say. Their time together in Vegas already seemed like a weird, prolonged, dream. Leslie would go back to work. Fran would see her family.

'Is this it then?' asked Leslie.

'I guess so.' Fran smiled and held out her hand. 'Thank you. For everything.'

'No no no,' said Leslie, batting her hand away. 'Not like that. You can't love me and leave me.' She got out one of her business cards, wrote her home number on the back, and handed it to Fran. 'We'll see each other while you're here in Vancouver. Call me.'

'Thanks,' said Fran, looking down at the card. 'Well. Goodbye.'

'Okay,' said Leslie. 'Good-bye.'

As Fran turned to leave, Leslie stopped her again. 'Wait,' she said, 'come with me in the taxi. I'll deliver you myself.' After a pause, it occurred to her: 'And where might that be?'

'My sister's office?'

'Your sister's office. Sounds good to me.'

'Are you a client?'

'Well,' said Fran, 'not really. I could be.'

The receptionist gave her a look. 'You'll have to wait.'

'Okay.'

Fran waited in reception for thirty-five minutes. The receptionist watched her out of the corner of one eye. People emerged from other offices, and went back in again, but not Fran's sister Sarah. Fran sat very straight and kept her handbag upright on her knees. Ordinarily, she thought, during a wait like this she'd be taking care of — amusing — Louis. Louis. She thought of his small body, and how he'd jump off the leather chairs and roll on the expensive carpet with a special glee. Louis. She felt herself moving forward, toward her regret, toward her longing. She backed up, pushing it away. I can't think about that. I can't think about him. I can't start missing him even more than I already do. Not yet. I'm not ready.

Fran and Sarah had been opposites as children, close in age alone, Sarah bookish, organized, Fran wanting Barbies and fairy wings and boys. Not even their mother's deterioration pushed them together; Sarah became more and more worried and involved, Fran more and more dismissive, distant, wanting to get away. And then, when they went to London, and Fran stayed behind, her distance became literal, real, and there was no reason whatsoever to pretend to get along, no need to try. I don't like her, Fran thought, and she doesn't like me.

Eventually, Sarah emerged from her office. She was speaking in earnest to her client as she led him to the door. She glanced at Fran and then looked away. Looked back again. There was an almost imperceptible hitch in her stride. She shook the man's hand.

'I'll call you the minute I hear anything.'

The man nodded. Fran noticed that he'd been crying.

He was gone. Sarah turned around and looked at Fran. She frowned and smiled at the same time.

'Is that why they pay you so much?'

'What?'

'Tissues and sympathy.'

'Frannie...' Sarah walked into her office. Fran trailed behind.

Sarah shut the door with a click. 'You are behaving very irresponsibly.'

'And hello to you too.'

'Nick is worried sick.' Sarah moved to her desk and began shuffling through paperwork, as though looking for the relevant document. The corner office had a panoramic view of downtown, the mountains, Stanley Park, the Strait, Lion's Gate Bridge. Fran looked around. Sarah had her own chrome-and-glass water cooler, and her own black leather settee.

'I know. We've spoken.'

'You've spoken, have you?' Sarah's tone was sharp.

Fran nodded.

'What the fuck are you doing?'

'I thought you'd be pleased to see me.'

'Louis isn't even two yet, he—'

'I know how old my son is.'

'Where have you been for the last ten days?'

Fran sighed. 'I don't have to answer your questions. I haven't been subpoenaed.' She walked toward the window, looked out at the city. The rain had stopped and the mountains were almost visible. Behind her, she could feel Sarah's impatience.

'The sky is never clear when I'm here,' she said. 'What's the point of mountains if you never get to see them?'

'We've had a lot of lovely weather recently. Vancouver is a very beautiful city.'

'So you keep telling me.'

'I don't have time for this, Fran.'

Fran turned toward her sister. 'Oh. Okay. I'll see you some other time.' She walked to the door.

'No. I mean— I don't mean that.'

'Yes you do, Sarah. You're a very important person.'

'Oh, fuck you, Fran.' In every aspect of her life, Sarah was calm, controlled, and disciplined. Except one aspect: her family. Five minutes with her sister and she was bilious with rage. 'No. I don't mean that.'

'Yes you do.'

At that moment, the door opened, and a man in a suit and tie walked in; his cologne followed close behind. He walked up to the desk and put his briefcase down, took off his suit jacket — releasing yet more cologne into the air — and placed it on a hanger on the back of the door. He looked at his watch and, still standing, flicked through the pages of the desk diary. He glanced at Sarah, who hadn't spoken, and then at Fran.

Fran could see her sister was blushing.

'How did it go, Larry?' Sarah asked.

The man smiled. 'A piece of cake. They rolled over, just like I said they would.'

She nodded. 'Great.' Then she spoke to Fran, as though they'd just met. 'Could you come through with me, please?'

She went toward a side door that Fran had assumed was a closet, opened it, and beckoned Fran inside.

Once Fran was in, Sarah reached around her and closed the door firmly. They were in a small windowless room that, in a former life, had indeed once been a closet. There was a small overloaded desk with a chair in front of it, the walls racked with document-crammed shelves. There was no room for anything else, not even a small framed photograph of Larry's view.

'Are you—'

'Shhh,' Sarah hissed. 'Keep your voice down.'

'—his secretary?'

'No. Of course not. I'm a lawyer.'

Fran looked around the tiny room once again. 'Well, you're not a partner, are you?'

Sarah was angry now. 'Nobody makes partner for at least a decade.'

'Okay,' said Fran calmly. 'So you're not a partner.'

'I never said I was a partner.'

Fran raised her eyebrows.

'I'm not a partner. All right?'

'I wouldn't care if you were his secretary, Sarah.'

'I'm not his secretary!' Sarah sat down and opened her laptop as though she intended to get back to work.

'I'll go see Dad. I'll stay with him.' Fran paused. 'Where will I find him?'

Sarah took a calming breath. Closed her eyes, opened her eyes, looked at her watch. 'It's Friday. He'll be working at home.'

Fran nodded.

Sarah looked at her sister. 'I'll come round tonight — tell Dad I'll bring some supper.'

'Okay,' Fran said, her hand on the door. 'Sarah—'

'Yes?' She tilted her chin forward, and smiled purposefully, back in character once again.

'Can you lend me some money for a taxi?'

I didn't mean to be mean. But I couldn't help myself. Sarah did that to me. She always did that to me; when I was around her I'd take up sarcasm and malice as though they were second nature to me. Having a baby turned me into a shouter; having a sister turned me into a bitch. Families.

Tony lived in the house that he and Ireni bought after he finished his master's degree and got his first proper job in the Geology Department — now Earth Sciences — at the university. At the time it was a bargain, even for East Van. Since then the neighbourhood had struggled to remain determinedly funky; when the Italian-run pool hall and coffeehouse was under threat from Starbucks, the local community had mounted opposition, signed petitions, put up posters. Their campaign was not successful and the coffee chain resumed its foamy saturation of the city. House prices in the area continued to rise, but there was enough low-rent accommodation around that the schools remained substandard, prostitution thrived, and the park was a wasteground of discarded needles, condoms, and shopping carts.

It was a beautiful little house, built in the thirties by an Armenian carpenter for his own family. Parquet floors, foot-high wooden skirting boards, carefully perfect architraves and windows, every inch meticulously finished, the kind of house that only needed polish to look perfect. Tony had added onto it after the girls arrived, an extra bedroom and bathroom in the eaves, but he'd done a good job of it, and kept the spirit of the original craftsman in mind. Ireni had loved the house: Tony felt the house was not the same without Ireni.

They met when he was teaching assistant at a university summer school in the Kootenays, supervising a group of undergraduates for six weeks. He was camping with his students near the river and every morning they commandeered the university bus to drive into town for breakfast. She was waitressing in the hotel restaurant, the only restaurant in town. Tony thought Ireni poured coffee unlike anyone he'd seen before; she held herself back somehow, different from everyone else in the room. He watched her carefully but couldn't bring himself to say much beyond 'with bacon', 'over-easy', and 'yes, please'.

One day, in the late afternoon, they ran into each other at the swimming hole, Ireni and her two girlfriends resplendent in the polka-dot bikinis they had ordered from the Eaton's catalogue without their mothers knowing. He was field-trip supervisor, so when it came to local girls, Tony figured he could have first choice.

Curious about local history, as well as most other things, Tony got straight to the point. 'Are you a Doukhobor?'

Ireni frowned; it was as though he'd seen right through her disguise. 'Why?'

'I'd like to know, that's all. I've never met one before.'

'You'd like to collect me, like one of your soil samples?' Ireni's friends giggled.

Tony was also wearing a bathing suit, and was a little uncomfortable with his own skinniness. 'Sure.'

'Not really,' she said, pointing at her friends, 'they're much more Doukhobor than me.'

Not long after that, Tony was commandeering the university bus all by himself, telling one group of students he'd be with the other group, while meeting Ireni elsewhere. He was accustomed to girls who took him so far and then pushed him away; free love hadn't yet made it as far west as BC. Ireni did not push him away. She'd seen something in Tony, something she thought she needed.

They got married in Vancouver in the autumn. She was eighteen, fresh out of high school, and he was twenty-three. Her parents didn't come; they sent money for the wedding but hadn't had enough to come themselves. Ireni could tell that despite their unrelenting drive to become ordinary Canadians they were disappointed that she wasn't marrying a Doukhobor boy. Tony's parents disapproved as well. He hadn't finished his master's yet, he hadn't been to Europe, he hadn't taken advantage of all the opportunities afforded him. As far as they were concerned, Ireni was British Columbia's equivalent of a backwoods girl, and from a strange Russian sect to boot.

'She doesn't wear one of those headscarves tied under her chin, does she?' Tony's mother asked. 'A pinafore? Clogs?'

'No, Mother,' Tony replied.

'Do you think she'll want to burn down our house?' Tony's father asked, smiling.

Tony didn't think this comment merited a reply.

He brought her to Vancouver, and she did her very best. She was young and pretty, with dark curls and dark eyes, no accent, a willing smile, and a spontaneous laugh that made everyone nearby want to laugh with her. 'Excellent posture,' was Tony's mother's first aside and he knew then that it would be all right.

And it was all right. They got an apartment on Cambie and he studied while she made ends meet; both activities were time-consuming. She was glad to have left the Kootenays. Ireni's parents had worked hard to get away from the past. They had taken a big step when they moved away from the farm and into town; Ireni's marriage and move to Vancouver was a great running leap further still. Before anyone noticed, a decade had passed. Tony had his doctorate, and his university job, Ireni had Frannie, and

Sarah, and the house built by the Armenian. It hadn't yet occurred to either of them that anything could go wrong.

Tony was in the basement, working on his project. It was his own project, nothing connected with his work at the university. He'd given up on telling people what he did a few years back; in the past it was only small boys who understood what the word *paleontology* meant, but that had all changed after *Jurassic Park* and its sequels, followed by Ross Geller from *Friends*. His colleagues were pleased, paleontology was sexy all of a sudden, and student numbers soared, like the Indiana-Jones-effect on archeology in the seventies. But he'd grown tired of having to deflect people's disappointment when he told them that he didn't do great big dinosaurs, that his specialism was a tiny Cambrian-period gastropod. Not only that, but he'd grown tired of the long-extinct snail himself, especially after Stephen Jay Gould published his geological blockbuster about the Burgess Shale and got it all wrong, however eloquently.

He liked teaching, he was a good teacher, it was his choice to do more teaching and less research, less work in the field, more time to take care of Ireni, but sometimes the university lecture hall felt a very long way away from the earth and its mysteries. Because he couldn't travel much, didn't like to be away for more than a few days, even now, just in case Ireni needed him — who was he fooling, in case Ireni turned up, which, in reality, she had stopped doing — he'd taken on more than his fair share of departmental paperwork, of sitting on boards and in committees. Truth be told, he'd stopped being a proper academic a long time ago and had become more of an administrator. That was okay, he told himself, he kept telling himself, he was bored with his subject anyway. But occasionally — very occasionally, like this morning in fact — he'd find himself wondering, was I really bored with pale-ontology or was it Ireni, Ireni's drinking, that diverted me?

Anyway, it didn't matter now, it was too late. These days, he was much more interested in the work of his colleagues than his own. One of his favourite projects in the department was the Galloping Glacier. It was a smallish glacier, up north in the Yukon, and every once in a while it moved very quickly. There were a number of these surge-type glaciers in both Alaska and the Yukon; back in the 1930s one in Alaska had moved three miles in three months. Tony's colleagues had their glacier wired up with instruments and they monitored it constantly. They were waiting. It last moved around twenty years ago, and they figured it was about due once again.

Still, Tony had his basement to console him. He was conduct-ing a survey, digging a test pit. It was complicated and involved a number of what to outsiders might look like large piles of dirt. But, in the basement, Tony was happy. He had his radio, his com-puter, and his project.

He'd started around the time that Ireni first took to disap-pearing, after they'd returned home from London without Frannie. He'd gone looking for her, but she didn't want to be found, and, back then, she'd turn up, eventually. When she was gone he didn't know what to do with himself, and his mother — a child of the Depression — had always said, 'When in doubt, work.' Tony had no lack of work, he usually had at least three papers and two reports outstanding, deadlines passed, as well as endless demands from students and colleagues, but with Ireni gone he felt the need for something more affecting than the sound of his own written voice.

For a number of years his progress with the project had been sporadic and very slow but, in the last twelve months, it had picked up speed. He'd dug up most of the floor of the basement. It hadn't been difficult. Initially he thought he'd have to hire a jackhammer and he was almost disappointed when he found that the thin layer of concrete broke up under his pickaxe like burnt sugar on crème brûlée. It was hard work, nonetheless, tough physical labour, but he liked to come down here and sweat his worries out, like a member of a volunteer chain gang. He hadn't found anything of interest, building rubble mainly, but it didn't matter. This was where he came to be by himself. This was where he came to think about Ireni. He could smash up the floor in peace.

That morning he had received a letter from the university outlining potential terms for early retirement. He couldn't remember why he had made the enquiry in the first place. Early retirement? What would he do? Spend more time down here? Harass his daughter Sarah even more than he did already? Sell the house, buy a Winnebago, and hit the road, drive south to the desert and see some real rocks for a change, instead of wasting his time on the overly business-like students that populated the campus these days?

He was fifty-eight years old. Fifty-eight, he thought, pushing the spade into the ground with his foot before hitting another stone. How did I get this old? What's happened to me? He stood, straightening his back slowly, and looked around the room.

And that was where he was when the doorbell rang.

He wiped his hands on his pants and made his way up the stairs. And opened the door to his daughter, Frannie.

When she was a little girl, they were pals, Frannie and Tony. Tony wasn't good with babies — he could pat their backs when they cried, but not much else — but he got better once they were big enough to be his little chums. He liked to take his girls on outings, one at a time, never together — they fought too much for that to be fun. Stanley Park, the zoo, the aquarium, the seawall, the beach, Granville Island, the art gallery; that way they could talk and he could spoil them. As far as the girls were concerned, it was great. Tony thought it a relatively foolproof method of parenting; he tended to forget it relied upon Ireni doing everything else that needed doing.

'Daddy!' Fran had decided to take the effusive, it's-so-good-to-see-you, line of defence. From the look on his face she could tell that her arrival was a complete surprise. Sarah hadn't told him anything; he didn't even know she had left London. She wasn't sure whether to feel relieved by that or not.

'Fran!'

They embraced. It was a big hug, a bear hug, they'd always hugged that way.

'You look the same,' she said, although it wasn't true. His hair was greyer and he was thinner. He looked less healthy, less well kept than he used to. 'Were you in the garden?' She was looking at his hands, the dirt caked beneath his nails.

'Ahh — yes,' said Tony, nodding. 'You look wonderful.' That

wasn't true either. Fran looked tired, too thin, and worried. He was always shocked when he saw his eldest after they'd been apart for some time, shocked to discover she was no longer a child.

Fran put down her bag and walked through the sitting room. It led to the dining room, which led to the kitchen, which opened onto a narrow deck overlooking a verdant, rather overgrown garden. Fran leaned on the railing, and took a deep breath. 'Vancouver always smells so green. It smells wet. Lush. Composty.'

'It's the rain.'

Fran laughed. 'The damned rain.'

Tony watched his daughter. 'Would you like something to eat? Are you hungry?' She sniffed politely, a gesture as familiar to him as his own face. 'I wish you lived closer,' he said. When they talked to each other it was as though they were continuing a number of unfinished conversations at the same time, from when she was six, when she was ten, when she was sixteen.

'When did you last see Mum?'

He frowned. 'Peanut butter and cheese sandwich?'

Fran made a face. 'I don't think I like those anymore.'

'No? I do.'

'Well, have one then, if you like. Sarah's bringing some food around later.'

'I bet she won't be bringing peanut butter and cheese sandwiches though.'

'No,' said Fran, 'you're probably right.'

Tony went back into the kitchen. He stood at the counter and talked to Fran through the open window. 'January?'

'That's six months ago!'

'Is it? Well, March maybe. I don't know.' As he spoke, he took the loaf of brown bread out of the breadbox and lined up the slices on the counter — three sets of pairs. He got the peanut butter, the butter, and the cheese out of the fridge.

'Don't you go and look anymore?'

'Yes. I do. That's how I found her. In March.'

Fran looked out at the garden. The lawn had become smaller over the years, the plants surrounding it, moving in, squeezing it out. Everything had grown huge, enormous dense and frilly ferns, very tall and voluptuous lilies, waving grasses with thick black stems, massive fleshy hostas beneath it all; it was like a primeval garden, carnivorous.

'Where was she?'

'Do you really want to know?' What he meant was: Do I really have to talk about it?

Fran walked into the kitchen. Tony had coated the bread with chunky peanut butter and was laying neat squares of orange cheese on top. She looked at her father.

'Gastown. Near the steam clock.'

'On the street?'

He nodded.

'Where was she living?'

Tony cut the sandwiches into four and piled them on a large plate. Then offered the plate to Fran. She took a piece and sat down at the table.

'I don't know.'

'Did you ask?'

'I don't know if I remembered to ask. I don't remember if she thought to tell me. I don't know, Frannie. I really don't know.'

Fran chewed her sandwich. The peanut butter stuck to the top of her mouth. The cheese adhered to her teeth.

He could see she couldn't speak. 'How long are you staying?'

She swallowed, took a drink to clear her throat. 'I don't know.'

Tony started, looking around the room as though he'd remembered something. 'Hey!' he said, 'where's my little boy?'

Fran sat up, not sure what he meant.

'Louis! Where's your baby?!'

Louis and I were fine. Just fine. We were getting on. I'd made all the arrangements, and they were working. Time had expanded and a week was like a year, ten days felt like a decade.

I hit a rough patch. I guess it was inevitable. At first I'd had all this adrenaline, adrenaline mixed up with fear. And when it turned out Fran wasn't dead or lying injured in some alleyway, I had adrenaline mixed with anger. Then there was the whole business of finding a way to survive on my own, on our own, without her. The arrangements, the endless arrangements. And after that, well, there was — nothing.

I was a single parent, on my own with a very small child. I would have been angry — I should have been angry — but I was too tired.

Claire was great. She helped out a lot. Even Celine took it upon herself to check if I was okay, dropping round a big bag of things from the organic supermarket every couple of days. But Claire was the one I relied on most: she took time off work in order to help fill the gaps in my schedule. And she helped me find the childminder, and reassured me that the whole set-up — Louis at the minder's in the day, in the restaurant in the evening — could work. It made me realize how important it was to have someone to talk these things through with, how much easier it is to make decisions about your child when you've got someone who can share the responsibility.

Claire and I quickly fell into a pattern of seeing each other every day. She'd often come to the restaurant at the end of the evening, in order to help me get Louis home again. And, once I'd got him into his cot, settled with a bottle, we'd sit together for a while, relaxing, calming down, having a bottle ourselves. More often than not, she'd spend the night on the sofa because she couldn't be bothered to go home; this was not in itself out of the ordinary as, over the years, Claire had slept on that sofa many times.

And it was great having her around all the time. In some ways it was almost like having Fran there. Claire and Fran and I had been close for a long time, and she and Fran were such good friends they had become, in many ways, very similar people. Claire knew the right thing to say to me, regarding Louis, regarding the complex arrangements I had made, the thing that Fran herself might have said.

One night we were sitting on the sofa watching TV. We had drunk a bottle of wine, a really good vintage that I had been saving. Claire kicked off her slingbacks and put her feet up on the coffee table. The nights were warm — unusually warm for London — and the windows were open and the flat was flooded with soft air. Claire was wearing a short skirt and I found myself looking at her legs.

Claire was a lot taller than Fran and she had long and lean legs. From where I was sitting they looked smooth and tan and, well, glorious. It would have been easy to reach over and run my hand along her calf. It would have been easy to move my hand up toward the soft part of her thigh. It would have been easy, Claire and I.

I met Fran in the corridor on her first day at school; we were fourteen. We started going out with each other almost immediately. We got married after we finished our A-levels and we have hardly been apart since. She's the only woman I've slept with. In fact, she's the only woman I've kissed. And I know the same is true of Fran; at least, I knew it up until ten days ago. I guess that makes us unusual in this day and age — we're like relics from a long-lost generation. Childhood sweethearts. I'd always found great comfort — satisfaction — in that phrase.

I'd been staring at Claire's legs for a while. I looked up, and Claire was looking at me, and I could see she knew exactly what I was thinking. I'd had too much to drink, I was tired, I was lonely. Fran had run away, leaving me unbalanced, punch-drunk. Claire and I had known each other for so long; Claire knew what I was thinking. That it would have been easy. That it would have made sense. That Claire was almost like my childhood-sweetheart-in-waiting.

Claire stood up. She leaned over me. Her hair brushed against my face. I could smell her perfume.

She kissed me on the cheek.

She put on her slingbacks, picked up her bag, and left.

And I knew that I had made a mistake. Claire and I — it would never be anything other than hideously complicated. I could have kicked myself across the room for being so stupid. From then on Louis and I would be that much more lonely.

The next day Fran rang me. She'd left Las Vegas and gone to Vancouver. This was good. In Vancouver there were people who would talk sense to her. When the phone rang, I knew it was her before I picked up the handset.

'How are you?' She paused. I was doing my best, trying not to get angry. 'How is Sarah?'

'She's okay. Works all the time. Has one-night stands with her married clients.'

'Sounds good.'

'She's not a partner.'

'Oh. So does that mean you like her more now?'

Fran laughed. The sound tinkled down the phone line and upset my stomach.

'Your dad?'

'I don't know. He doesn't say much. Just spends his time making me sandwiches.'

'Oh.' I paused. Took a breath. Could I ask when she was coming home? 'Have you seen your mum?'

'No. We don't know where she is. Sarah and Dad haven't seen her in months.'

'Months?'

'I think she's got much worse. She doesn't come home anymore. Ever.'

'Not even for money?'

'No.'

Neither of us spoke for a moment.

'Fran? Is that why you left?'

'What do you mean?'

'Your mother. Disappearing.'

'You mean I'm turning into her?'

'What? No. That's not what I mean.'

Her voice caught, as though she was about to cry. 'I am like her, aren't I?'

'No, don't be ridiculous. You're not an alcoholic. You're—' I stopped myself. I couldn't believe I was trying to make her feel better about leaving. 'Just come back. Come home.' My tone was a little more wheedling than I intended.

'I can't. Not yet.'

'But you will?'

'I have to go. I'm going to go now Nick. Good-bye.'

She put the phone down. I picked it up and threw it across the room.

After that, things didn't go so well for me and Louis.

He had a cold. I'd been giving him kiddies' vitamin C and pumping him full of orange juice and carrots and kiwis all week, but the virus was relentless. His cold got heavier and heavier. The usual little boy thing, two continuous streams of bright green snot snaking down below his nose and a noisy cough. I kept sending him to the childminder because he was still cheerful and busy despite his condition. He was prone to wiping his nose with his fist and rubbing his eyes, and that morning I noticed he'd developed conjunctivitis; pus was leaking out of the corners of both his eyes. We went along as usual to the childminder but she took one look at him and shook her head. He'd infect every child he came in contact with.

I put in a call to Gina and took Louis off to the doctor's surgery, waited for ninety minutes to be seen — that was fun — and picked up the prescription. Got to the restaurant at twelve o'clock to discover that we were fully booked for both lunch and dinner that day.

Over the last four hours Louis had gone from his usual ebullient little self to a weepy and clingy thing. He wouldn't let me put him down, he wanted to be held the entire time, and he would not go to anyone else, not even his favourites amongst the staff. His eyes were hurting and his nose was streaming and he spent much of his time with his face buried in my shirt, using me as a kind of man-sized tissue. So I carted him around the place, I had no choice, and customers oohed and ahhed at him, which made me feel embarrassed — I hate it when people use their kids as glorified accessories, and I hoped no one thought this of me. I tried not to think of the germs he was spreading.

After lunch I took him home and he had a nap. At six we headed back into the restaurant. He was a little bit more cheerful and willing to let go of me. We embarked on his routine — Alice read him a couple of stories while I sorted out his bed and made his bottle.

'I think he's got a fever,' she said when I picked him up. And, indeed, in the space of twenty minutes he'd gone from slightly under the weather to feverish and dopey. 'I'll put him to bed,' I said, 'he needs to sleep.'

I put him down and he curled up with his bottle and closed his eyes right away.

Two hours later I was out on the floor talking to some regulars, a couple who lived around the corner and came in at least once a week. Alice interrupted me.

'He's coughing.'

'Yes?'

'No, Nick, I mean, he's *really* coughing.'

I stood outside the door to my office. Inside, Louis wasn't so much coughing as honking, like a big goose with a sixty-a-day habit. In between honks, it sounded as though he was having trouble breathing.

I opened the door and picked him up. Turned on the light to have a look. He continued to cough hard, the sound coming from deep within his little body. I patted his back, wiped his face with a damp kitchen towel. His eyes were gummed up, almost glued shut. He could hardly breathe, his nose was so snotty. He was hot, and sweating.

One more great cough and he threw up all over me, all over the floor, all over his own little bed. I held him with my arms outstretched, trying hard not to throw up myself. He threw up again, all over my desk. I squatted down on the floor with him, and he threw up once more, all over Gina's feet; she had come to the door to see what was happening. The smell was overwhelming.

'Fucking hell,' said Gina. 'Does his head spin round as well?'

And Louis did what babies do after they've thrown up repeatedly. He smiled as though he'd never felt better, and laughed at me crouching there on the floor beside him. He'd managed to throw up on everything, apart from himself. I was too appalled at the state of my suit to move. Louis, smiling happily, got up and toddled out into the dining room.

I was covered in puke and unable to step out of the office for fear of contaminating the kitchen and shutting down the entire restaurant.

Louis, on the other hand, had discovered the pleasures of the dining room in the evening.

When Sarah finished work, she went into Urban Fare, picked up some food for supper, and got in her car to drive to Tony's. While making a right-hand turn at a red light, she cut in front of a cyclist who fell off her bike and onto the sidewalk. Sarah left the car straddling the corner and got out. The rider was up off the ground, and shouting: 'What the fuck do you think you're doing, why the fuck didn't you look in your mirrors, you didn't even fucking signal, who do you think...'

The cyclist's words washed over Sarah's head in a gentle wave, muffled, indistinct. In place of her own usual version of road rage, Sarah felt nothing. Ordinarily she'd be happy to shout back at the cyclist, regardless of who was in the wrong. The rider was not wearing protective gear, not even a helmet, and last time Sarah had seen her she had been riding on the sidewalk. But Sarah couldn't muster a single obscenity. Her sister Fran was here, in the city. They were going to have to talk about Ireni.

'You're okay,' Sarah said calmly. 'Your bike's okay. I'm okay. We're both okay.' She got back in her car and drove away.

Sarah hadn't made partner before the age of thirty, even if that's what she let her sister, and a few others, think. She hadn't exactly lied about it; it was more a case of what they wanted to believe. She was thirty-one now, and she'd be lucky if she made partner by forty. Maybe non-equity, if she played her cards right, made lots of money for the firm, won lots of cases, raised her profile, didn't offend anyone, didn't get married and go on maternity leave. And she wasn't all that well paid. It was a decent salary, sure, but not like what people think. She was a single woman, unencumbered; it was easy to look like she had lots of money. If you ironed your shirt, cleaned your shoes, took care of your nails, and used expensive make-up and good hair products — no frizz, absolutely no frizz, whatever the occasion — anyone could look expensive, well maintained. She didn't have tons of natural style like her sister Fran; Fran could wear a garbage bag and look sexy. She didn't have a husband, nor a boyfriend, couldn't remember the last time she'd been on a date (yes she could: Joel Barnes, two years ago, they had sex, she regretted it, and refused his invitation to go to a mud bath spa in California for the weekend). She didn't really have friends either, there hadn't been much time what with law school, and trying to get ahead, and Ireni. She couldn't help it if she looked like a successful lawyer; she'd looked like a successful lawyer since she was sixteen. Getting the right look took time, and planning, but it was worth it. She found that people bought the image, wholesale.

She wasn't sure how she'd ended up in family law either, it wasn't what she intended. She'd wanted to be a criminal lawyer, like in the movies, or a corporate litigater, something flashy and expensive. The kind of lawyer that people hate. Instead she found herself handling the divorces and custody arrangements of the firm's business clients and, worse, the other lawyers. People hated that kind of lawyer as well, but less passionately: divorcing couples had each other to blame and despise.

Larry, the guy in the big office next door — *her* office — was an asshole. He was married to another of the partners, a high-flyer called Linda who billed at least twice as much as him every year. He had only hit on Sarah once; he won a case on which she'd done much of the work, and after it was over he took her out for a celebratory drink. They went to one of the trendier bars downtown, and he put his hand on her knee. Mild, really. She lifted it off and said, 'Sorry, Larry'. In an effort to recover himself, he told her he really respected her, and now that was one of his favourite phrases, used on the frequent occasions when he thought she didn't know what she was doing, when he thought she was about to make some colossal error of judgement. 'You know how much I respect you, Sarah,' he'd say, 'but. . .' Then he'd spell out what an inexperienced, unintelligent, idiot girl-head she was being.

It wasn't easy. Sarah jogged, she roller-bladed, she power-walked on the seawall, she went to the gym. She had a one-bedroom condo in Yaletown with a view of the water if you leaned out at a ninety-degree angle from the far end of the balcony. She bought it at the top of the market, but that's okay. She spent time with Tony. She and her father were close; together they had weathered Ireni. She liked living in Vancouver; in the winter she skied at Whistler when she could afford it and went hiking in the summertime. She knew hers was a good life. And still, 95% of the time — 99%? — she was angry. At Larry. At Ireni. At herself. At Fran.

How had Fran gotten away with it? How had Fran gotten away with getting away so completely? They'd left her behind in London, it was true, but Sarah had always assumed that was temporary, that Fran would come back to Vancouver, back to the family, one day. She'd come help out with Ireni; she'd have to see that they needed her help with Ireni even if they didn't — couldn't — ask for it. She'd bring Nick with her, that went without saying, but Nick would be happy in Vancouver, he'd be perfect for the Vancouver restaurant scene.

But Fran hadn't come back. She'd stayed in London, which as far as Sarah was concerned, was a big grey city with a crumbling infrastructure and no redeeming qualities. She'd left Sarah on her own with Tony, on their own with, and without, Ireni. She'd missed out on the whole fucking drama of it, and Sarah had had to take on what should have been Fran's share of the responsibility. And it ruined things for her. Fran's not coming back ruined things, she thought, she liked to think. And now Fran is back, in this ridiculous situation, having spent ten days in Las Vegas with some woman she met there, having run away from her husband and her child. It was incredibly fucking annoying.

Sarah stopped at yet another set of traffic lights. When the light changed to green, she pushed the accelerator to the floor and roared across the bridge, toward her father and her sister.

Ireni. Sarah and Tony stopped trying to rescue her at the same time, without talking about it. Three years ago: Tony had gone on one of his routine hunts for his wife. He found her downtown, brought her home and called his daughter who came round as soon as she could. Together, they cleaned her up. Tony helped her in the bath; Sarah cooked a meal.

'Ireni,' Tony said as he and Sarah watched her eat. His voice cracked. Sarah looked away in order not to see the pain on her father's face; Tony looked away in order not to be seen. Ireni kept on eating.

'Will you try now? Are you ready?'

'Ready for what, darling?'

'To stop drinking. To stay home with me?'

Ireni looked from her husband to her daughter and back again. 'Of course, darling. I wouldn't dream of leaving. I'm home now. For good.'

Looking back, Sarah knew right there and then that this was

not true, that she was lying again, but, like Tony, she elected to believe it, she continued to want to believe her mother's promises, as though gripped by a waning, but still compelling, religious faith. But the fact was her mother only ever said these things, made these promises that weren't really promises, to please Sarah and Tony.

The next day Sarah went to work. Tony was supposed to go into the university for a faculty meeting. 'You go, Dad,' Sarah had urged over the phone, 'you'll only be gone a couple of hours. She'll probably sleep.' In the past, one of them would have stayed home to police her, but now they'd moved beyond babysitting Ireni.

Tony went into the bedroom. Ireni was still sleeping soundly on her stomach, face buried in her pillow. The room stank; Tony opened the window. 'I won't be long,' he whispered to his wife.

When he returned at lunchtime, Ireni was gone. He put his briefcase down on the table. And took a decision to do nothing.

Sarah rang that evening.

'She's gone,' Tony said.

'What did she take?'

Tony hadn't thought to look. 'I don't know. Not much, if anything.' He'd taken some change out of his pocket and left it on the kitchen counter that morning. From where he stood he could see it was still there.

'Oh.' Sarah paused. At that moment, she also decided to do nothing. 'I'll come round in a couple of days.'

They hung up their phones, Tony in his house, Sarah in her condo. At the same time, they sat, Tony on a kitchen chair, Sarah on her sofa. They were too worn down to feel anything.

Later on, Tony got up and went down to the basement. Sarah went out for a run along the harbour.

And now, pulling up in front of her father's house, Sarah wondered what the next few days would bring. I don't want to get out of the car, she thought. I don't want to have to go in there and pretend to be happy, to make out as though everything is fine, two loving sisters spending an evening with our loving daddy.

She stared at the street, the street she'd grown up in, the street she'd walked to school down, rode her bike on, watched her sober dad drag her drunk mum along kicking and screaming. She shook her head. She'd go into her father's house now, and be nice.

Fran woke up in her old bedroom, the bedroom she'd left behind when the family went to London. Her father had changed it over the years, very slowly; every time she visited, it was a little more guest room, a little less her room. She didn't mind. It felt like a good thing to her, healthy. Not like with her mother; the house was still full of Ireni. Tony hadn't put any of her things away. Her jacket was still hanging on the hook in the kitchen; Tony's closet was full of her clothes. The perfume she used to wear still sat on the dresser, her toothbrush in the bathroom cabinet.

Fran got up, went down to the kitchen, and found a note from Tony. He was at the university all day; she could reach him on his cell phone. Sarah was, of course, at work as well. She hadn't stayed late last night; they ate the food she brought with her and talked about — well, Fran thought, nothing. The weather, the new mayor, Tony's students, Sarah's clients. Nothing. Fran stepped outside onto the deck. The sky was low and grey, the air cool; it wasn't raining, not yet anyway.

She had a piece of toast. She made coffee. She took a long shower. She painted her toenails. She ironed her linen dress and put it on. She read everything of interest in her father's copy of the *Globe and Mail*. She listened to the CBC on the radio; they were burbling on about a man in Winnipeg whose dog could bark along to the national anthem. It was like every other visit she'd made to Vancouver.

In her father's house Fran felt very young and very old at the same time. Young, as though nothing she had done in her adult life, nothing she might have accomplished, had any relevance here. Old, like she'd been making these visits for years and years and years, and nothing would ever change. Except things did change. Ireni. Louis.

Outside, it had started to rain.

Inside, she got up and went toward the stairs, thinking she'd lie down again. She stopped at the door to the basement. A voice in her head said 'Don't go down there,' but she went down anyway.

It was dark. The steps were filthy; she could feel dirt crunching underfoot. She moved along, sure she could remember where the light switch was, relying on her bodily memory of the house. The air was cold and it smelt powerfully basementy — drains, and mildew, and below ground-level moisture. As she stepped forward, the sound of gravel skittering down the stairs in front of her echoed hollowly, as though she was entering a cave.

She found the light switch.

And the light revealed: a huge hole where the basement floor had been. It took a few moments to understand what she was seeing. It was like a building site, except, confusingly, inside a building. There were great mounds of dirt where her mother's drying racks and ironing board and storage chests had once stood. Building rubble was banked up around the furnace in the far left corner, and there was a great teetering earth wall opposite. A plank led from the foot of the stairs where Fran stood across to the other side of the room. Over there, Tony's workbench remained intact, a PC on one end, his tools neatly stacked on the table, hanging from their hooks on the wall. Beneath the plank, the centre of the room was now a great, deep pit.

The hole was at least ten feet across and, Fran thought, ten feet deep. Ten feet, that is, to where the water level had risen. She stood on the plank, looked down, and saw her own reflection.

I've got to call Nick. No, I can't call Nick about this, he's not going to want to hear about this, he wants me to come home, he'll want to know what the fuck I'm doing, and why the fuck I'm staying away. I can't call Nick about a hole in the floor of the basement.

Claire. No, I'll have to tell Claire all about what has happened to Ireni. She'll be upset that I've never told her before and, of course, she'll be upset about Ireni as well. Then she'll get upset about Tony and the hole in the basement, and then she'll get upset with me.

I'll call Sarah. No, this is too big, it's too soon — maybe she knows already. Maybe she thinks this is normal. Maybe she — I'll call Leslie. Leslie will know what to do. Leslie will know what to say.

After the taxi dropped Fran off at her sister's office the day they came back from Vegas, Leslie felt at a loss. She'd asked the driver to take her to her apartment in English Bay, but then she told him she'd had second thoughts and asked to be taken down to Kitsilano. Leslie intended to go for a walk on the beach, but when they got there she remembered she still had her bags with her. So she asked the driver just to stop for a while. He got out of the car and lit a cigarette. 'Vancouver's last known smoker,' Leslie said. 'Yeah,' he replied.

The beach at Kits is domesticated, a city beach; there's a playground with swings, and benches along the grass verge. The beach itself is strewn with driftwood, like all the beaches along the coast here, strays that have escaped from the log booms that the tugboats drag into the harbour. By Vancouver standards it was a warm day, but the air felt cool and moist to Leslie after Vegas, and the sky was low and grey. She used to come here nearly every day with Charlotte, even in the rain.

After sitting for a while, looking out at the enormous freighters waiting to enter the harbour, she told the driver she was ready to go. She asked him to swing round in front of the houses behind the beach before heading up the hill. He drove slowly, as though he knew she had something on her mind.

There it was: her big old house.

A couple of years before they had Charlotte, Leslie and David moved for the tenth time in as many years; one of the perks of Leslie's job is seeing houses new to the market before anyone else. This time round they bought a big old wooden house a few blocks back from the beach. It had been completely renovated by the previous owners. The ground floor was open plan, with polished wood floors, there was an oak staircase that lead to a mezzanine floor; off of which were several large bedrooms, each with its own ensuite. A balcony overlooked the sitting area with its grand stone fireplace. At the back, glass doors opened onto a large cedar deck and garden. It was like a luxurious old ski chalet, but in the city.

When Charlotte arrived, the open plan of the house was a real boon. In the evening, after she'd gone to sleep in her room, Leslie and David could sit in the front room and still hear her if she cried. And once she was walking, the balcony was a great source of amusement; she liked to run away from them, up the stairs to where she could taunt them from overhead. Leslie was forever calling out 'Charlotte, where are you?' only to have her reply, 'Up here, Mummy! Up high!'

The banisters on both the balcony and the broad staircase were very sturdily made, the struts close enough together to prevent little bodies slipping through. To Leslie the house felt profoundly child-friendly; Charlotte loved nothing more than to slide down the stairs on her rump and run around and around the ground floor, like a tiny manic circuit-trainer.

They were devoted to her. They were both surprised and rather thrilled to find themselves with a child. Leslie was forty when she got pregnant; having a baby hadn't really occurred to her before then. She was focused on her career throughout her thirties and David, well, he was a geologist and, Leslie thinks, geologists are not like other people. But after her fortieth they said to each other 'Why not?' and Leslie spent the rest of that year pregnant.

Leslie was good at being pregnant. She ate well, she didn't drink, she kept fit and healthy. She didn't go to Las Vegas. Not once. Not even one last fling. Her old gambling buddy, Barbara, who already had three kids by then, two of whom were teenagers, was disappointed in her. 'If we don't go to Vegas now,' she said, 'who knows when you'll get another chance?'

Leslie tried to reassure her. 'Soon enough.'

But Barbara remained dismayed. Leslie thought Barbara preferred it when she didn't have children. Barbara had given up work to start a family and Leslie thought Barbara felt it was unfair that she should have both a job and a child.

Leslie doesn't see Barbara anymore. Leslie's getting pregnant and refusing to go to Vegas that year was part of it, but Barbara had already started having the operations. So when Leslie had Charlotte at the ripe old age of forty Barbara was appalled that she wasn't interested in even the tiniest amount of reconstructive surgery. 'Help,' was what she called it. 'Wouldn't you like some help, Leslie?'

'No, Barbara, I'm happy. I'm going for the lived-in look. Pre-owned, as they say.' Barbara wanted to give her a gift voucher for her favourite clinic in Seattle as a post-natal present, but Leslie told her not to waste her money.

And yet, after Charlotte died Leslie found herself wishing she had accepted those gift vouchers that Barbara wanted to give her. She could have gone to that surgeon and asked him to cut out her heart; she had heard that those doctors will do anything for a fee. She could have taken it home and offered it to David on a plate.

Leslie was a good mother. She did all the right things. She was loving and giving and involved, and she knew when to stand back, and when to say no, and when to celebrate. She could handle Charlotte's temper, her passions, her fears, she was happy to take care of her when she was sick, she didn't even mind it on the few occasions when Charlotte told Leslie she was mad at her. And David was a good parent as well, Leslie thought. He took being a father very seriously, and she would never forget watching him watch her, his face imbued with joy.

Charlotte fell off the balcony in Leslie's big old house by the beach. She'd got beyond the age when it occurred to them to worry about her on the stairs. She was a tall little girl, growing taller every day; pants that fit her one minute were up around her ankles the next. And it was as though living in a house with a balcony had inspired in her a love of heights — wherever her parents were, Charlotte liked to be higher, highest. Leslie figured she'd been climbing onto the balcony rail for some time, but she never actually saw her up there. At four, Charlotte didn't know much, but she knew enough to understand a bit about what was allowed and what was not. Leslie's guess was that she climbed up onto the rail to sit or, better yet, stand. And that something happened. She lost her balance.

Leslie walked into the room as Charlotte was halfway between the balcony and the floor. She hadn't cried out and her fall was silent, apart from a curious swooping sound as she moved through the air.

And then she landed, with a terrible smack.

As Leslie ran over to where Charlotte lay, she expected her to leap up and run off, laughing. But she did not. She did not get up again.

Charlotte died. And with her, everything. Leslie, David, their marriage. They were dead too, but they had to carry on living.

And the next year Leslie made more money than ever. But who cares? Leslie thought. How could anyone care about money?

When Fran rang her the day after they got back, Leslie went round right away. Much to her surprise, she missed her; she woke up in the night and was surprised she wasn't there in the next bed.

Fran's father's house was lovely and Leslie couldn't help but see the collateral it represented, once Fran told her how long he had lived there. 'If your father ever wants to sell...' she said. Fran smiled and nodded, and took her down to the basement. Leslie thought she was being taken on a tour of the house.

They stopped at the bottom of the stairs.

'You did tell me that your father is a geologist, but I'd forgotten.'

'A paleontologist in fact.'

'Yes.'

'Well,' said Fran, 'can you tell me what this is?'

They stood and stared at the hole for a long while, amazed by the weirdness of it, by the strange spectacle. They didn't hear

Tony come in the house. They didn't hear him until he was on his way down the stairs.

'Hello, Fran,' he said.

'Oh, hello, Daddy,' she replied. 'This is my friend Leslie, who I met in Las Vegas.'

'Hello,' her father said evenly, 'thank you for being so kind to my daughter.'

'It's nice to meet you, Mr—' Leslie stopped. She still did not know Fran's surname.

'Call me Tony.'

'Okay, Tony.' She couldn't think of anything else to say.

'Well,' he said. 'Can I make you girls a cup of tea?'

Fuck it, thought Tony. Fuck it.

He hadn't wanted Frannie to see the hole in the basement; he hadn't wanted anyone to see that hole. That hole was like a dark secret — who was he fooling? that hole was a dark secret — and you don't want anyone to know your dark secrets.

He doesn't know why he started to dig, he just did.

Tony felt like he was trapped between shifting tectonic plates; how's that for a crass geological metaphor, he thought. That's me, there. I've fallen down the crack, between two continents. When the plates move, they won't even notice me. I won't be squashed flat; I'll be pressed to nothing, instantly.

He couldn't stop Ireni from drinking. That failure had defined the last twenty years of his life. He had believed he could do it, he had tried every argument, every treatment, every clinic, every trick he could think of, but he couldn't make it happen. Sarah tried her best as well, but they might as well have been trying to persuade the moon to go away. They couldn't do it, not together, not apart.

And he did mind the fact that when they left London, Frannie stayed behind. He knows now — now that she's here with him once again — that it was a mistake to break up the family in that way, that it was part of their own very personal catastrophe. She talked him into it, he let her talk him into it. She said it was best for her education; she'd do her A-levels. He assumed what she meant was that she'd do her A-levels in London and then she'd come home to Vancouver to do her degree. But he knew she wasn't all that interested in education; he should have known there and then that wasn't her real reason for staying.

Tony understands now that he allowed Fran to stay in London because part of him thought it might be easier to cope with Ireni that way. How could he have thought that? he wonders. He was panicking about the situation, and it felt logical at the time: it would be easier to deal with Ireni without Fran, he and Sarah could sort out Ireni. Sarah was — is — much more like him than Fran had ever been. They have the same way of doing things, methodical, studious. Frannie was like Ireni. Gorgeous, yes, and unpredictable. Full of mystery. Some people are mysterious, there's no doubt about it, while other people just aren't. There's nothing mysterious about me, thought Tony — maybe that's why I'm digging that hole, a desperate bid for my very own elusive quality.

Was he saying that he preferred one of his children to the other?

Where's that bolt of lightning?

For a long time Frannie looked as though she had battened down the hatches on the dark part of her character, the thing that made people close to her sit up and wonder how well they really knew her after all. She was a good wife, a good worker, a good mother. Then, she ran away. Tony knew that Ireni's drinking was nothing if it wasn't a kind of running away. He didn't believe Ireni meant to run away from him, more that she was running away from her own past, her own history. But the reality of it was that, when she drank, she abandoned him. And Fran's running away from Louis and Nick showed how like Ireni she was. Tony knew Fran was not about to turn into her mother, he knew that she would not start to drink. He felt sure she'd go back to Nick and Louis, eventually. But running away from her infant child — she did it because of Ireni, Tony thought. And because she was Ireni's child. And because of the mess, the huge fucking mess that he'd made of everything. And because he let her stay in London and he did not keep her close beside him.

Fuck it. Fuck them all. Oh, he didn't mean Frannie, or Sarah, or even Ireni. This was how he coped. He dug his hole. He used colourful language when he thought no one could hear him. He made disgusting cheese and peanut butter sandwiches for his dinner. None of it did the slightest bit of harm to anybody.

When Tony married Ireni, his Doukhobor girl from the southern interior, he thought she would come with a Russian clan alongside her, like a large chorus, ready to accompany them on the great occasions of life — wedding, babies, tenure — ready to help celebrate their achievements. But there was no Russian clan, not even one small bowl of borscht. Instead, Ireni was determined to fit into Vancouver, never getting it quite right, like a kind of wrong-footed chameleon turning red when she should have been green.

There was no point in hoping his wife would come back to him now. He continued to hope anyway. When Ireni stopped raging a few years back, he knew it meant she had stopped caring, stopped fighting with herself, stopped fighting. When the rages stopped, he missed them. They were like a big ugly teenage boy covered in pimples and melancholy; you can't wait for him to leave, but once he's gone, you find you are lonely.

She used to wreck the house. She did it in a controlled manner; she'd get absolutely plastered and she'd destroy a room. One room only. One room, trashed magnificently. The kitchen was first. Then the bathroom. The family room. The bedroom. Never the girls' rooms, thankfully. But every other room in the house. She always did it when she was alone, during the day when the girls were at school. Not that often — maybe once a year, later once every six months. The girls managed to avoid ever seeing her at it; Tony guessed that was part of Ireni's plan. He figured she never intended that he see her at it either, but he came home in the middle of it on three occasions. The first, in the family room — his scalp split open when a vase she threw happened to hit him. The second time, in the kitchen, when a chair she was trying to smash broke his arm. The third time, she was in their bedroom and he did not attempt to intervene but went down to the basement instead. He stood at his workbench and listened as she played herself out. After a while, he went upstairs to make sure she was okay.

But when he saw what she'd done, the damage inflicted on their room, the room he'd loved her in for all these years, he got angry. He shouted at her: 'What are you doing, Ireni?'

'I don't deserve this,' she said, quiet now, her speech slurred.

'What?'

'All this—' she swung her arms wide. 'This lovely house. My beautiful life.'

'But it's our home, Ireni. We've worked hard for it.'

She sat on the floor. 'It was my fault. It was my fault they took him away.'

Sasha. Her cousin. Tony knew there was nothing he could say.

Marriage is composed of a whole range of types of silence. There is comfortable silence — that's the good one, Tony thought, the one all couples must hope to achieve. Then there are the other silences: fearful silence, bored silence, aggressive silence, presumptive silence, weary silence, preoccupied silence, guilty silence, why-won't-you-listen-to-me silence. Ireni and Tony had their share of all of these. She never really talked to him about the rages, how they were inspired, how they might be assuaged. She hadn't the words for it. She couldn't explain.

But he knew why. She blamed herself for Sasha, Sasha's life as well as his death, in fact. He killed himself, eventually, after a long battle with his mental health. He was pretty crazy, Tony thought, Cousin Sasha. They'd taken him away to residential school when he was a little kid; Ireni had blamed herself for that, always. Then they'd turfed him out six years later, when he was nearly fourteen. He never recovered. And, Tony knows now, neither did Ireni. That's why she drank. What happened to Sasha made her drink. It made her drink and, Tony thought, the drink made her rage. And when the rages stopped, Tony lost his wife to the street.

The boys were off somewhere, trying to catch snakes. That's all they ever did in the summer, Ireni thought, all four of them running along the dry, twiggy slope by the side of the highway out of town, carrying big sticks, chasing the breeze as it moved through the grass. Sasha caught a snake last year, right here in the backyard, much to everyone's amazement. He held it up for everybody to see, two fingers pinching it behind its head, as though he'd been a professional snake-handler in a former life. The snake was long and slim and pale green, and it opened and shut its mouth slowly, like it was struggling to speak.

This year Ireni stayed at home when the boys went out snake-hunting. She didn't want to run through the brush, getting her legs scratched to pieces. She took her pink bedspread from her bed and two winter blankets from the airing cupboard and went outside. She dragged the folding deck chairs together and made herself a secret cave. She went inside and wrote KEEP OUT in large letters on a piece of paper, then put that, her library book, and a glass of water on a tray.

Inside the secret cave it was hot already but she didn't mind. The world was muffled and faraway. She read her book for a little while, drank her drink. Then she fell asleep.

When she woke up, Sasha was lying beside her. He was on his back. She began to speak, but he shushed her and pointed up to where he was looking.

There, on the pink ceiling, sunlight piercing through the tiny holes, were three daddy-long-legs. Very still, not moving. Ireni held back a shudder and a shriek.

'Be still,' Sasha whispered, 'or else they'll start dancing.' Dancing is what those bugs do — wild dancing, like the grownups late at night, like the floor is hot, they've had too much to drink, they don't know what they're doing. That's why daddy-long-legs are so awful — you never know when they might come at you. One minute they're over there, dancing, the next they are all tangled up in your hair. Again, Ireni worked hard to hold down a shudder and a shriek. She moved closer to her cousin and they stayed there for ages, watching, until her little brother John ran into the backyard yelping like an Indian and scalped the ceiling off the secret cave, carrying the daddy-long-legs away.

After Leslie and Fran and Tony made their way back upstairs, Tony made tea and they chatted, as though the hole in the basement did not exist. Leslie and Fran made a plan to meet up in a few days, and Leslie went back to work.

Sarah arrived. 'There's nothing to eat,' she declared, standing in front of the fridge. 'I'm hungry.'

'I'll make us something,' said Tony.

Sarah looked at her sister. She still had not asked why it was that Fran had left Louis and Nick, why it was that Fran was sitting at their father's kitchen table.

Fran looked at Tony. They had not discussed the basement. They had not talked about Ireni.

Tony looked from one daughter to the next. He did not want to talk about anything. It was too much. It was all too much for him. They were like airplanes stuck in a holding pattern, forever circling each other, careful not to collide. He'd got used to a quiet life, on his own, with his project. 'Why don't you girls go on through to the family room?' he said. 'I'll make us something.'

'They don't have family rooms in England,' said Fran.

'They don't?' said Tony.

Fran shook her head. 'The houses aren't big enough.'

'That's not true,' said Tony. 'There are big houses. I've seen them. The Fitzgeralds'.'

'But they don't have family rooms. They don't call them that.'

Sarah snorted. She had heard enough. 'Do you think there's some kind of significance in that?'

'She speaks with a Russian accent now,' said Sarah.

'She does?' Fran replied.

'It's so annoying. "Darlink!" Like Zsa Zsa Gabor or something.' They were in the family room, lying on the floor in front of the TV.

Tony came in, carrying a large bowl of popcorn.

'Thanks, Dad,' said Fran.

'Every time I've seen her over the last few years,' said Sarah, 'her accent is stronger. Last time I saw her she kept talking about Sasha.'

'Sasha?'

'Her cousin. You remember.' Sarah looked at Tony for confirmation. 'She kept saying she needed to find him.'

Fran looked blank. 'I thought he died.'

'He did,' said Tony. 'He's dead.'

'He jumped off the bridge,' Sarah said. 'Lion's Gate Bridge.'

Tony nodded. 'That's right. When they found his body he had documents on him that identified Ireni as next of kin. The police came to our door one morning; I've never seen your mother more frightened. It was as though she thought they had come to take you two away.'

The police came early, first thing in the morning, before anyone in the house was awake. Ireni's parents were unprepared; her mother thought they had come to ask questions about Uncle, like the other times. Sasha was staying with them, he'd been with them most of the summer, and school had only started that week. The grown-up voices woke Ireni and when she walked into the kitchen, all the adults turned to look at her.

The tall policeman spoke first. 'Where's your Cousin Sasha?'

'He gets to sleep on the porch with my big brothers,' Ireni said crossly, and as she spoke she looked at her mother who for some reason was shaking her head, no, no, no, and frowning. The other policeman went to the porch, straight through the house, without hesitating. Ireni's parents stayed still, unable to move. Moments later they heard Sasha's voice.

It was Ireni's fault. If she'd said he wasn't there, if she'd said she had four brothers, not three — he was like a brother, he was more like her brother than her real brothers could ever be — if she'd told the police officers to go away, it wouldn't have happened. She knew without asking that that's what her parents had said to the police, that until she'd walked into the kitchen that's what they'd been saying. We have four sons and one daughter. Four boys. They all go to school. We are good people.

The policemen took Sasha away with them. Nobody fought, nobody struggled. It was the law — Sasha had to go away to school. Ireni stood at the front door with her family and watched the police car drive away. Her mother was beside her, crying silently.

Sasha could have come with her to school, her parents had been trying to persuade Uncle and Auntie all summer. He'd be behind, but he'd catch up quickly, Ireni knew that; Sasha was smart, smarter than her. Instead he was gone. And it was her fault. She'd given him up. He'd been taken away.

And now they had the job of telling Sasha's parents that their son was gone. Ireni's father drove up to the farm by himself that morning.

Her parents did not take Ireni to see Sasha at the school up at New Denver, not once during the six years he was there. She wrote to him every week to begin with, long letters stuffed with news, everything she could think of, but he didn't reply. She saw a photograph, she isn't sure where or when, and now this photograph has become her memory of that time; two women, dressed like Auntie, on one side of the fence, a boy, wearing a coat just like Sasha's, looking up at them from the other side. The women are crying, one glancing back angrily at the camera; the boy looks puzzled. On the snowy ground next to him sits a box; Ireni wonders what his mother has brought for him. Food maybe. A Doukhobor Bible. They never offered to take her to visit, and when she asked, they said no. She was ashamed at her own relief. She was afraid that if the police saw her outside the wire fence, they'd take her inside as well.

The arguments grew louder and louder in the night, whenever Uncle and Auntie were there. 'You've got to agree to it!' Ireni heard her father shout on more than one occasion. 'You can't let them keep your child.'

'I'm not letting them keep my child, you idiot,' Uncle replied,

'I'm not...'

'Maybe it's for the best,' Ireni heard her mother say.

Silence. Ireni knew they were all looking at her mother.

'At least this way he'll get a proper education,' her mother continued. 'Learn English.'

More silence.

Ireni heard a woman — Auntie — begin to wail.

Not long after that — maybe Ireni fell asleep — she heard the sound of people leaving. She got up and looked out the window; the night was black and there was frost inside the glass. She saw Uncle and Auntie on the footpath. In times past they would have stayed the night. It was a long drive back to the farm, the heating in their car was broken, and there had been a lot of snow in the last few weeks. As she watched the headlights come on, Ireni wondered if Uncle was using the pink farmer's gas once again.

The floor was very cold, so Ireni pulled on her socks, and went into the kitchen. Her parents were still sitting at the table.

'How could you say that?' her father said to her mother as she entered the room. It was as though they could not see her.

'If they agreed to the schooling, they could have Sasha back.'

'But that's not the point— it's not the—'

'What makes you think it won't happen to the rest of us, to our children?'

At that, they both looked at Ireni. And continued to speak as though she wasn't really there.

'Our children go to school. We live in town. We are law-abiding.'

'We're Sons of Freedom though. Aren't we? Everyone knows that's our family.'

Ireni's father blinked, as though he'd suddenly seen his child standing there; he reached out and drew Ireni close to him. It's my fault, Ireni wanted to say, but she knew that if she said it her father would deny it, even if it was the truth. It's my fault, Ireni said to herself, Ireni kept on saying.

The years passed. Ireni grew up, and so did Sasha, but not together. When Sasha was released from the school six years later, he came to live with Ireni's family, enrolled at Ireni's high school. Ireni had a bedroom to herself now — her big brothers had both left home, chasing work across the country, it was just her and her little brother John left now — and up until the day Sasha arrived her main worry was that she'd have to share her room with him. But she discovered that it was worse than that; in the years that he'd been away, Sasha had become a stranger. He'd grown, like her, but that wasn't it. He wasn't the Sasha that Ireni remembered. He had changed on the inside as well as on the outside.

Uncle and Auntie drove down to see Sasha on Saturday afternoons. Both families crowded into the small front room; Ireni's mother, who had adopted yet more Canadian customs, served milky tea and scones. The men attempted to talk farming while Ireni's mother came and went with cups and saucers, napkins and butter knives. Ireni curled up on the daybed and read her way into a book, away from the scene. Sasha and John were stiff-necked inside their good collars. Auntie tried unsuccessfully not to cry. Sasha sat next to his mother, although somehow not beside her, and did not speak. 'More tea?' Ireni's mother shrieked as she moved into the kitchen yet again.

He was silent most of the time; he made his bed every morning as soon as he got up and when they sat down for meals he ate very quickly, as though he was afraid his food would be taken away. Ireni was nearly fourteen now, and interested in girlish things; she was learning to sew her own clothes and she had friends in the town and she was good at school. She looked at Sasha across the breakfast table, and felt wary.

But during the warm summer months of the year that followed, she and Sasha got up early most mornings, to be first in the water before it got too crowded. They didn't play on the rope swing — they were too big for that — Sasha no longer shouted in his big Russian voice; he no longer had any accent, he no longer used Russian words. But they swam together, and raced each other, and floated on their backs, looking up at the blue sky.

He left school as soon as he turned sixteen. When Ireni asked where he was going, he said, Vancouver. The big city.

A few years later, when Ireni met Tony and he said he came from Vancouver, she too was on her way.

Ireni found Sasha a number of times during her years of searching. Once, in the seventies, she came across him by accident. Frannie and Sarah were little girls, she'd taken them to the beach for the morning. It was early — Ireni still liked to get down to the water before anyone else had got up. The girls were scrambling over the driftwood when they found a sleeping man wedged between two logs. Their shouts brought Ireni running and woke the man.

It was Sasha.

'Ireni?' he said, shaking sand from his beard. The girls looked from their mother to the man, wide-eyed.

'Sasha?'

He nodded, and then smiled. 'I'm a crazy person now,' he confided.

Ireni looked down at the girls. 'This is my Cousin Sasha. You don't know him. Go and play.' But they ignored her. Sarah, who was only one, took hold of Ireni's leg.

'I was diagnosed last year. I'm on medication.'

Ireni nodded, as if this meant something to her. 'I'm married. I have two children. My husband works at the university.'

Sasha laughed. 'Sounds lovely.'

Ireni smiled back. 'It is.'

'Do you see the families?'

Ireni shook her head. 'I don't go back.'

'Me neither.'

He stopped smiling, and took a deep breath. He stank. Ireni pushed against her urge to back away. 'Okay,' he said. 'Well, I'll be seeing you.' He picked up the bag he'd been using as a pillow, waved at the girls, and walked away.

Another encounter, years later. It was after they'd returned from London. Frannie had stayed behind in England; Sarah was out for the evening with her friends; Tony was away at a conference in the US. The doorbell rang. Ireni remembers, because when she got up from where she was sitting in front of the TV, she knocked her glass tumbler off the arm of the chair; it fell onto the coffee table and smashed. The wine — Calona Red — flowed across the table, under the stack of magazines, onto the carpet. The doorbell rang again, reminding her why she was standing.

She opened the door to Sasha. This time he was clean-shaven. He looked sixteen once again.

He smiled his Sasha smile. For a moment, she felt warm water on her skin, and wished they were swimming.

'You're drunk,' he said.

She nodded.

'I've come to say good-bye.'

She stepped back and opened the door wider, hoping he would come in. It was Sasha — Sasha! — she could talk to him. He would understand.

Every time she found him he was that much worse off. He was depressed, he was schizophrenic, it was a chemical imbalance; he was on the right drugs now, he was in a clinic, the drugs weren't working, he was off the drugs, he'd been hospitalized. He had his own place, he was living in the street, he was in a hotel, he was in prison.

And here he was, at her door. Sasha — the boy of her dreams, her warm summer dreams. It was her fault he was sent away. It was her fault that her cousin was crazy.

'You must come in. You must come in and talk to me.'

'No.' He shook his head. 'I've come to say good-bye.'

She'd had a lot to drink. Now she was angry. 'But you never come, all these years — you never come and visit—'

'You never came to visit me.'

'I've tried. I've looked for you, but I never know where to find you…'

'I mean then. Back then. You never came.'

'They wouldn't let me! I was a child.'

'So was I. Look. It doesn't matter. None of it matters. It's over. Finished. I'm done with it.'

Ireni was awash with guilt. 'I didn't know what to do— I was seven years old— I—'

Sasha took her in his arms. 'Are you always drinking?'

She leaned into his chest. She nodded.

'You shouldn't, you know.'

'That isn't going to stop me.'

He didn't argue. He held her tightly. After a while, he released her, and stepped back under the front door light. 'Okay,' he said, 'okay, Ireni. Good-bye.' And he turned and walked down the footpath and out onto the street.

Ireni watched him leave. He looked tall and strong, straight-backed and capable. Wherever he's going, she thought, he'll be all right. He'll be okay.

It wasn't until the next morning that she began to wonder why he had come to say good-bye and what, exactly, that might mean. The police came to her door late that day.

RETURN

Fran!' There was so much to say, Claire was having trouble speaking into the phone.

'Are you okay?'

'Me?' Claire thought of the nights she'd spent on Nick's sofa, she thought of what had almost happened and how she'd hardly seen him since. 'I'm fine.' Pause. 'And you?' Claire wondered, should I tell her to come home, should I ask what I can do to help, should I tell her I miss her? Or should I just tell her off?

'I'm okay,' Fran said.

Another pause.

'How are they?'

'Who?' Stupid question, Claire knew.

'My boys.'

'They're fine. Absolutely fine. They are doing just fine without you.' Oh fuck, thought Claire, why did I say that? That's not true.

Another pause. Fran could tell that Claire wanted to punish her, but she didn't mind. She deserved it.

'They're not fine. Fran, what the fuck are you up to?'

'I couldn't keep doing what I was doing.'

'What do you mean?'

'I can't not work, and I can't stay at home with Louis all the time. I love Louis— you know I love Louis— I—'

'How is running away going to solve anything?'

'It was either that or— I don't know— there wasn't much choice. It was either leave, or leave. Nick couldn't listen to me. He couldn't hear me. I couldn't talk to him.'

'He'll listen to you now.'

'You think?'

Claire wasn't sure. 'Well, you shouldn't count on him waiting for you forever.' It was a low blow, Claire knew.

'What?'

'He's a bloke, isn't he?'

'What do you mean?'

'Oh, never mind.' Claire tried another tack. 'You've got to come back. Louis is going to forget who you are.'

'Oh Jesus,' said Fran, and she burst into tears.

'Oh Fran, I'm sorry, but come on, it's true. You're his mother, for fuck's sake. He needs you.'

'I'm his mother,' Fran repeated. How could it be that after all this time, nearly two years, it still didn't feel real?

They said good-bye. In London, Claire opened the windows in the main reception room of her parents' big Georgian house and lay down on the floor.

In Vancouver, Fran sat on her father's sofa in the family room. She felt too tired to cry. Who could she talk to? She couldn't keep bugging Leslie. She picked up the phone and dialed her sister and, miraculously, got through directly.

'Nick's having an affair and Louis has forgotten me,' she said.

Sarah, facing the windows and Larry's view of Lion's Gate Bridge, was dismayed. 'Frannie,' she said, 'what are we going to do with you? Eh? What are we going to do?'

'I never understood why they let you stay in London.'

Fran and Sarah were walking to the beach. Fran looked at her sister. 'You wanted to come back to Vancouver.'

'I know I did, I'm not talking about me.'

'They let me stay because I wanted to stay. I was going to do my A-levels—'

'I know, but doesn't it seem odd to you now, with a little hindsight? Especially given Ireni's own experience of broken families, and children being sent away to school.'

'It was completely different, Sarah. You know that. There was Nick, we had to be together, obviously we were meant to be together. It made sense.'

Sarah decided against pointing out that, recently, Fran had left Nick. 'I know, I know all that. But you were sixteen. It's — what, 6000 miles? — from London to Vancouver. Eight time zones. Ten-hour flight. Think about it. Maybe Ireni thought she had to lose a child, to compensate for the loss of Sasha to her family.'

Fran walked. Sarah accompanied her. She thought about it. And sighed. 'I see what you mean. But I wanted to stay. I belong in London, Sarah. It's my place. Anyway,' she said, 'it was good for me. It was our mother who got herself into trouble.'

'You're right about that.' Sarah paused. 'It's like there's another version of our family out there somewhere — you and Nick came back to Vancouver with us, Mum pulled herself together and joined AA, I got married and had myself three or four children—'

'Sarah, you're only thirty-one, you sound like you're an old woman full of regrets.'

'But I am,' she said, 'that's exactly what I am — an old woman full of regrets.'

Along the sidewalk the concrete slabs were broken and uneven, as though a subterranean creature had tried to force its way up and out. The two women watched the ground carefully as they walked.

'I hated you for staying.'

Fran could not look up, for fear of tripping and falling.

Sarah continued. 'I hated you for getting your way, for having Nick, for being allowed to grow up so suddenly and completely.'

'I know.'

'And it was terrible when we came back here. Those years with Ireni — all through high school and university and law school — you can't imagine what it was like for Dad and me. And you missed it all. You were not here.'

They dropped down off the sidewalk and onto the sand. Sarah headed for the water, taking off her sandals so she could get her feet wet.

Fran spoke first. 'I think part of me knew what was going to happen.'

'How?'

'I'd seen enough TV movies. Alcoholic housewife. No happy endings.'

'Oh. Well, you could have told me. Maybe I would have stayed in London too.'

Fran took off her heels.

'I knew it couldn't get much worse when I started to like it after she disappeared,' Sarah continued. 'It was a shock to discover how dismayed I was every time she came home.'

'That's awful, Sarah.'

'I know. Horrible, but true. Life was — is — easier without her.'

'Fuck. I hope no one ever says that about me.'

Sarah laughed. 'Well, I'm sure that's not how your husband feels.'

There's this thing out there, thought Fran. She was lying in the bath in her father's bathroom, which was cluttered and homey and full of unused gift boxes of bath salts — did I give him all of those? she wondered — and unopened bottles of Old Spice. There's this thing out there, and it's called a Bad Mother. And it's wild and wicked and it shouts and screams and it harms little children and it wants its own way and it's always tired and it wants to be alone and it fucks up boys and turns them into serial killers and fucks up girls and turns them into Bad Mothers and... And it's me.

And it's Ireni.

Fran knew about Ireni. She knew about her childhood, she knew about Sasha being taken away, she knew about Sasha dying. She'd been told these things, by her father when she was younger, when she had been looking for explanations. But, despite knowing about her mother's past, she had never thought about it all that much. Why not? She wasn't sure. Self-defence? Maybe; she had to have some way to ward off the guilt she felt over her mother's drinking. It was her fault, surely, that her mother drank; she mocked herself for thinking this while continuing to halfway believe it. Self-absorption? Quite possibly. Fran knew it was convenient for her not to have to think too much, too often, about Ireni. But, she wondered now, where had it all led to, all that not remembering, all that not talking, all that not thinking? To a succession of bathtubs — first at home in London, and when that no longer worked, Las Vegas, and then here in her father's house, far away, too far away, from her son, Louis, and her husband, Nick.

She turned on the hot tap once again.

'She liked to sunbathe. When we were kids. We'd come home from school and find her in the garden, lying on a deckchair. With a big G&T, lots of ice. Reading a novel.'

It was a glorious blue-sky-clear-mountain-vista Vancouver day, perfect for driving around the city, viewing houses. In the last couple of days Leslie had been busy catching up at work, trying to reassure all her colleagues and clients that she hadn't suffered some kind of real estate–related breakdown. She was fired up, full of energy after her long break, and she made a couple of big sales straightaway, the commissions large enough to cover her Vegas losses, plus some. Sometimes, Leslie thought, I ask myself what to do with all my money, but then I go ahead and book another trip to Vegas.

She'd picked up Fran from her father's house and now Fran was sitting in the passenger seat of her car. She was wearing her linen dress. She was staring hard out the window, talking about her mother.

'Slow down. Here. Slow down,' Fran said.

Leslie couldn't see who or what Fran was looking at. They were driving through the boarded-up streets of the downtown Eastside and the sidewalks were crowded with people. 'It must be cheque day,' Leslie said, 'when the welfare payments come through.' The street people were out in force, dealing drugs, turning tricks, standing up, falling over, giving each other diseases thought long since obliterated: the opposite of Vancouver's smiling tourist face.

Leslie sincerely hoped Fran would not find her mother here.

'Nope. Keep going.' Fran sat quietly for a moment. 'Did you divorce David because Charlotte died?'

Away from the darkness of the room in Caesars, it was a little harder for Leslie to talk about her girl. She gripped the steering wheel hard and then spoke. 'I guess so. But I didn't divorce him. We divorced each other.'

Fran kept staring out the window.

'He was a geologist, after all.'

'Did he dig a hole in your basement when the world got too much for him?'

'No.'

She looked at Leslie. They both laughed.

Earlier that day Fran rang Leslie at her office and asked if she could take her out for a drive. Leslie told her assistant she was going to see a client. Maybe that's what Fran was after all, Leslie thought, a client. A good real estate agent is a kind of therapist or, better yet, horrible phrase Leslie thought, a life coach. She was helping Fran sort out her life; it was a role in which she felt comfortable. Only without the house purchase her client 'relationships' usually entailed.

'She'd get really brown in summer. Like you. Lovely and golden. Like I used to. I guess I got that from her.' Fran shook her head. 'Bad for the skin.' She was watching the street, the pedestrians, as they drove. 'My sister Sarah, so good at absolutely every-fucking-thing else, would burn in a minute. Blisters. Peeling. Getting a suntan is the one thing that I can do better than her. Of course she tries to make a virtue out of having 'sensitive skin', but it doesn't work. My mother and I used to lie in the sun together after school, and Sarah hated that. My mother was useless at a lot of things, but when it came to lying in the sun and downing the drinks I mixed her, she was great.'

Now Fran fell silent, scanning the crowd, which was beginning to thin. 'But she's not so bad, my sister. Not really. It's odd. You think you know someone, then they turn out to be someone else entirely.'

'Where to next?' Leslie asked.

'I don't know. Last time Dad found her in Gastown.'

'Okay. Gastown it is.'

Leslie had never liked Gastown. It's the oldest part of Vancouver, but it fell into disuse decades ago as the focus of the city shifted away from the harbour. The city had tried various schemes to smarten it up over the years, attempting to promote the old buildings as funky and, failing that, pretending it was groovy, but it's too far off the beaten track, and has remained tacky and unloved. Neither Leslie nor Janet Brushhead had managed to shift the tone.

They were driving through the end of Gastown, where even ultra-cheap and nasty touristification has failed, where the wampum shops merge into the rough-looking bars and poisonous cafés that managed not to get knocked down the year the city hosted Expo and tried to pretend there were no poor people in BC. There was a consignment clothes shop, and Leslie was sure there used to be a decent shoe shop — 'I don't shop much,' she said to Fran, 'but I try to be observant, these things have an effect on property values, after all' — but the rest was derelict. Including the people. They drove past the Edwardian, one of those seedy old Vancouver hotels that has been there since the town was a log-jam on the river.

'Stop the car,' Fran said.

There was a woman sitting on the steps in the entrance to the hotel. She was clutching a bottle in a brown-paper bag, surrounded by garbage bags that Leslie assumed contained her worldly goods. One of her arms was in a sling. A wino, standard issue, thought Leslie.

'That's her,' said Fran. 'My mother.'

Leslie pulled the car over. Fran was sitting very straight-backed in the passenger seat, staring out the window. She was holding her Caesars Palace shopping bag on her knees.

'That's her there?' Leslie could see the woman in the rear-view mirror.

Fran nodded. They sat for a while longer. For once, Leslie could not think of a single thing to say. They watched a polystyrene cup blow across the street.

'What's in the bag?' Leslie asked.

Fran looked down at it, as if she had forgotten it was there. 'Food. Clothes. One of her old sweaters. A copy of *Great Expectations*.'

'*Great Expectations*?'

Fran nodded again. 'She read it to me. When I was little.' She did not move to open her door.

'Do you want me to come with you?'

Fran sighed. 'Yes, please.'

They got out of the car and walked down the block. Leslie half-expected Fran's mum to have disappeared. But she hadn't. She was sitting there, in the hotel doorway.

Leslie stopped a few paces before Fran and watched. Fran stood in front of her mother, and her mother looked up, shielding her eyes from the sun with her good hand. She was either suntanned from living outdoors, or brown-skinned with dirt and city filth. 'Got any change, darling?' she asked Fran.

Leslie watched Fran fish round in her pocket. It dawned on

her that she probably wouldn't have any money. Leslie got a fifty-dollar bill out of her purse. Fran looked at it, looked at Leslie, and then gave it to her mother.

'Sarah always used to say I shouldn't give you money. She says you'll just drink it away.'

The woman on the steps looked up at her daughter. Leslie couldn't tell if she recognized her or not.

'It's one of the many things we disagree on,' Fran continued. 'What's fifty dollars when you see your mother only once every three or four years?'

'Gee,' her mother said, 'thanks, mister.' Her voice carried a heavy Russian accent. She shaded her eyes again. 'Hey,' she said, and Leslie could smell her breath from where she stood, 'Frannie. It's you.' She smiled. She pushed a couple of her garbage bags to one side, creating a little space next to her on the stoop, and patted it invitingly.

After a moment, Fran sat down next to her mother. Ireni squinted at Leslie now. 'Is that you, Sarah? Both my girls?'

'No, Mum. This is my friend Leslie.'

'Come and join us,' Ireni said. Leslie wasn't very keen on this idea. She was in the middle of a working day and the concrete didn't look all that clean. But she did as asked and took a place on one of the lower steps.

'Leslie,' said Fran, 'this is my mother, Ireni.'

Ireni held out her hand and Leslie took it. Ireni smelled, she really did. But then she smiled and Leslie realized with a start, she must be only a few years older than me.

'How are you, Mum?' Fran asked. 'What happened to your arm?'

Ireni took a swig from the bottle in the paper bag, and offered it to Leslie. She declined. 'It'll do you good,' she said, cackling in advance of her joke: 'It'll put hair on your chest.'

She turned to Fran again, without offering her a drink. 'How's your sister?'

'Oh, she's okay. She's doing well. Taking care of Dad. Still a bitch though,' Fran said.

'Now Frannie, you be nice to her. She's not too bright, you know.' At this, they both laughed.

'Listen, Fran,' Leslie said, 'why don't I go for a little walk? I can meet you somewhere—'

'No,' said Fran firmly. 'We need you here. Please.' She turned back to her mother. 'Have you got a place to go at night?'

Ireni nodded, but from the way she looked at the steps they were sitting on, as though she was about to offer to show them round her lovely home, Leslie's guess was that she was lying.

They sat in silence then. All three women turned their faces to the sun.

'The park,' Ireni said, after a while.

'The park?' said Fran.

'Stanley Park. I go there. It's better. Cheaper. Not so many crazy people.'

'Oh,' said Fran and, after a moment, 'that's nice. We like the park. Don't we?'

Fran looked at Leslie. Leslie nodded her approval.

'You never ask for anything,' Fran said to Ireni. And to Leslie: 'She never asks for anything.'

'Apart from loose change,' said Ireni. She waved the fifty-dollar bill at them, gleefully.

'Okay, Mum,' Fran said. 'Don't spend that all in one place.'

'Thank you,' said Fran's mother, with immense and sharpened dignity, 'thank you for coming to visit me.'

They sat and talked for a little while longer, small talk about nothing important — the weather so far that summer, the cruise boats Ireni had seen in the harbour, whether there were more tourists, or fewer tourists, this year. She showed them her Pacific Tours bag and they admired it. She didn't ask any questions, and Fran did not ask any either. But Fran did offer her mother one piece of information: 'I had a baby,' she said. 'A little boy.'

'You did?' Ireni said, and for a moment Leslie saw a flash of the other Ireni, the old Ireni, the mother, the wife.

'Yes,' Fran smiled. 'He's at home in London with Nick. He's called Louis.' Fran paused, momentarily stricken, but she shook it off. 'You're a grandmother.'

Ireni looked at Leslie. 'Have you seen him?'

'No,' she said. 'But I'd like to.' Leslie saw herself then, on a plane to London to visit Fran, to meet Nick and Louis. Maybe it was possible, she thought, to make a different kind of family. Maybe there were other ways to spend her money, something beyond the fake desert oasis, the neon, the imported palm trees. Well, she thought, London will make a change from Vegas.

'He's pretty sweet,' Fran said. She reached in her handbag and took the photograph out of her wallet.

'He's so cute,' Ireni said, 'look at him.'

'You can keep it,' said Fran, 'I've got plenty.'

'Thank you, dear,' she said. She placed the photo carefully inside one of the garbage bags and, for a moment, looked pleased that they had found her. But when she looked up once more Leslie thought it was as though the other Ireni — briefly glimpsed — had slipped away. 'Have you got any change?' she asked.

'No, Mummy, we—' Fran said, about to explain. She stopped herself and looked at Leslie.

'Maybe it's time to go,' Leslie said.

Fran nodded. Leslie could see she wasn't able to speak.

They said good-bye. Fran hugged her mother. Ireni, who no longer seemed to recognize her daughter, allowed herself to be hugged.

They got in the car and drove away.

What was it like for Fran, Leslie wondered, finding her mother on that doorstep? Leslie saw winos all the time downtown; it had never occurred to her that a homeless drunk could be somebody's mother. She used to wonder how they survived, especially in winter, but not how they got there, the route taken through life. Picking up Fran in Vegas was the closest she'd ever come to one of those people, and that's not very close.

Fran's mother turned out to be a small dirty person with matted grey hair sitting in the entrance to a hotel frequented by junkies and hookers and, well, people like Ireni. Later, Leslie wondered if she should have offered to take her back to her place, given her a bath and a meal, some more cash, clothes. Oh well, Leslie thought, I can always go back and find her another day.

Afterwards, on the drive to her father's house, Fran talked.

'She's so calm. As if nothing could be more natural; as if all is right with the world and she's in a beautiful place. It's like she's a kind of homeless drunken saint.'

Leslie thought of disagreeing, but did not.

Fran paused. And started up again. 'I don't understand how she ended up this way. They spent years trying to save her. They tried everything, AA, Alanon, ACOA, intervention, counselling, hospitalization. Sarah even tried to get her committed one year, but my father wouldn't let her. Now they do nothing. Tony used to give her money, but not anymore. That's it. He's given up. He says it's her life. And you know, I never knew what to think before. I stayed away. But now I think he's right. The trouble for most drunks is once they give up drink, they find there is nothing to replace it. People drink for a reason, not just for the love of drink. My mother has her reasons. Take the drink away, the past is still there. Anyway, if my mother quit liquor now, I'm sure her body would give up and she'd die; booze is the only thing keeping her in one piece. And it's not as if she's hurting anyone apart from herself.'

Again, Leslie thought of disagreeing, but did not.

She drove Fran home. She offered to go in with her, in case her father wasn't there, but Fran declined.

'What are you going to do now?' Leslie asked. She meant today, but also tomorrow, and the day after that.

Fran shrugged. 'Go home.' Leslie wasn't sure if she meant her father's house or London, but it didn't seem right to ask. Fran leaned over and gave Leslie a kiss.

And Leslie drove back to her office where there were stacks of messages and three people waiting to see her.

That's it. That's my mum. That's Ireni. I've seen her now. I gave her the picture of Louis; now she knows that Louis exists. She knows that she's a grandmother, and I'm a mother. My mother was a good mother until I was eight years old and she started to drink. My mother was nearly eight the day the police came and took Sasha away. Sasha killed himself, and he took my mother with him. She is bound to him; that is her story. But it's not my story. I've got a life, in London, and I'm going to have to find a way to live it. We — Nick and Louis and I — are going to have to find a way.

This is Ireni: Fran can see her. She's thirty-two years old, same age as Frannie today. She is hosting a faculty party for her husband Tony; she is the only woman there without a job. Without an education. She feels ignorant, unable to contribute to the conversation. Nobody wants to talk about her girls; to tell the truth, she doesn't want to talk about her girls either. People compliment her on the food, but she knows it isn't all that good, she is not much of a cook. Or a hostess.

She excuses herself in the middle of a one-sided conversation with geophysicist Barry Brown. She picks up her drink. It's rum and Coke. A double. Sweet and tingly. Lots of ice. She carries it with her up the stairs. She goes into the girls' bedroom. She adjusts their covers, one after the other, Sarah, the youngest, first, then Frannie. She leans against the wall.

It was her fault that they took Sasha away.

She lowers herself to the floor. She hugs her knees and clutches her drink and begins to cry.

Frannie, awake, keeps very still under the blankets as she listens to her mother weep.

After Leslie drops Fran back at her father's house, Fran shuts the front door and stands still, listening. There is no one at home; Tony is at work, Sarah is at work, Ireni is on her concrete doorstep. The house is quiet. A car passes in the street. Quiet again.

Fran walks through the house, opens the door to the basement, and steps down the dirty steps carefully.

Nothing has been altered since her previous visit. She crosses the plank — it is sturdier than it appears — to her father's workbench and flicks on the fluorescent bar he uses to light his work area. She notices the computer has been left on, so she moves the mouse. The screen comes on. The image of a bridge forms itself, a traffic-cam view. She peers at it. Oh yes, she thinks, Lion's Gate Bridge. Sasha's bridge. Then she turns back toward the hole.

It really is deep. But that is it, that's all there is to see; the brighter lighting offers no further clues. Fran wonders whether she should ask her father about it, but it feels too private — she shouldn't be down there. Prying. She'll tell him about finding Ireni; he'll want to hear about that. She'll tell him about visiting with Ireni, giving her money. He'll be relieved.

Listen to me. It was not — NOT — that I thought Fran should-n't go back to work. I knew that not working was making her unhappy. I knew that getting out of the house was important to her well-being; I knew that. But we did our figures — we did them over and over again — and her working could not be made to pay. It couldn't. That's the truth of it.

But now that she's gone, I see there is another truth, buried under all my attempts at creative accounting.

Claire said it. She said it first. 'You didn't want her to go back to work, did you?' We were standing in the National Gallery in front of *The Bathers*. I'd taken Louis in to see her; this was about ten days after the incident with the legs. We hadn't seen her since.

'What do you mean? Of course I did, but we couldn't—'

Claire held her hand up in the air. 'I know all that,' she said. 'But the fact is that you did not like the idea of someone else — anyone else — taking care of Louis. You thought he was too lit-tle not to be with Fran.' She turned to catch Louis before he had a chance to smack the Seurat.

'Claire, that's not—'

'Oh grow up, Nick. There's nothing wrong with feeling that way. But it might have helped if you'd been able to admit it. And look at him—' we looked at Louis who was on his way toward another Old Master — 'with a childminder part of the time and perfectly happy.'

'He loves it.'

'See?'

So there it is, the plain truth: I wanted Fran to be at home with Louis. I wanted it, but I couldn't admit it. Is that such a terrible thing?

My job is to make sure that everything is running smoothly. I want people to have a good time at my restaurant. Even though it isn't top-league, Michelin-starred haute cuisine, I want the food to be memorable, and for people to feel glamorous and well-taken-care-of while they eat. People go to restaurants to be seen, and they go to restaurants to conduct private, intimate scenes and, in a good restaurant, the two things are not contradictory. It's like going to the cinema or reading a good book; much of the experience is in our imaginations. One of my waiters used to come into the kitchen and announce, 'And now, starring at table number nine, The Bitch From Hell,' or 'The Love-sick Couple,' or 'The Lonely Single Guy.' And he had it right; people come to restaurants expecting to star at their own table. And we, the staff, make that possible.

And you know, I used to think that all of this was incredibly important. I'd lose sleep worrying about the limescale on the tap in the sink in the ladies, or a new waiter whose manner I didn't like. For the past fourteen years Twenty-One has dominated my life to the exclusion of most other things and people. Not Fran, of course, and not Louis — I say that, and hope I sound convincing. But everything else. Everyone else.

But now, that's all changed. Since Fran left, everything has changed. I do my job and I do it as well as ever. But I see it for what it is.

I run a restaurant. If it closed tomorrow, it wouldn't matter one bit. People would lose their jobs, but they'd be snapped up within days, other establishments are always trying to poach my staff anyway. Regulars might feel a little disappointed, but London is full of good food these days. Another business would take over our premises — it's a prime location now. Within months — weeks even — it would be as though Twenty-One never existed. There would be no ripple effect. There would be no change in the breeze.

Fran is gone. I want her back.

I've got a plan. I've made a plan. It's going to work.

In her father's house that afternoon, Fran lies on her old bed, in her old room. She's gone around and removed all final traces of her teenaged self, found a box to store the few remaining souvenirs and knick-knacks, gone through her old clothes. Now she lies on her back and stares at the ceiling. Quiet. Too quiet. No one calling her name. No child shouting 'Mummy'. No Louis, no Nick, no Claire, no Celine, no London outside, heaving with life. What has she done? What is she doing?

The Galloping Glacier started to move yesterday. There was a lot of excitement in Tony's department, a lot of toing and froing. It travelled ten centimetres, which, for a glacier, is really quite something. Tony rang Sarah. 'It's to do with the glacier's drainage system,' he said. 'It's got poor plumbing.' A pool of meltwater builds up between the glacier and the ground that it rests on, building and building until, whoosh, the glacier shoots away on its very own waterslide. Tony's colleagues predicted it would pick up speed quickly. They were hoping that the data they collected would provide new insights into climate change. That, and into the Galloping Glacier itself, of course. 'I'm tempted to go up there myself and have a look,' he said to Sarah. He felt as though he'd been waiting for this for a long time.

No one in his family — Tony's tiny family — knew much at all about his working life. Not even Sarah. Back in the days when it was all going well, he and Ireni never talked about his work; she let her lack of education get in the way. He used to try to get her to go with him on field trips in the province, to hike up to the Burgess Shale sites, go visit the university dig, travel to Italy to see the Botticelli Gorge. But she didn't want to go. Outside the office, the department, his world of work remained private to him. These days Tony didn't really understand what his daughter Sarah did, what the law meant to her, what her workdays were like. This is part of what keeps everyone separate as people, he thought, separate in our jobs, separate in our houses. We have these spaces between us, Tony thought, literal spaces — you in your car, me in mine. Talking wasn't enough, talking wasn't compensation. Words couldn't bridge the gap, bring everyone closer together. We need something else. Proximity. So that we don't have to be alone all the time.

But I can't ask my daughter to live with me, Tony thought. That's just crazy. As crazy as my basement project. As crazy as Fran running away. As crazy as Ireni.

Or can I?

'I wonder if Daddy would be interested in me moving back into the house for a while.'

'What?' said Fran. 'You're kidding.' They were in the car, out for a scenic drive. Sarah was determined to make Fran like Vancouver.

'No— I— I don't know. I worry about him. He's lonely. And I don't find living by myself all that entertaining. It would only be temporary, I wouldn't sell my place, just sublet, three months maybe, six tops.'

Fran thought about the hole in the basement. 'I don't know, Sarah—'

'Oh, I know people will think its weird, but who cares. I'd like to live in the house for a while, I love that house, maybe help him clear Mum's stuff away. We could put it all in the basement.'

'Or maybe the attic,' said Fran.

'Wherever. It's time to clear it away. You know, his closet is still full of her stuff.'

Fran nodded. 'I know. The whole house is full of her.'

'I'm not saying get rid of it, just clear it away. I think it would be a good thing for us to do together.'

'You get on well,' Fran said, and suddenly she knew it didn't really matter any more if Sarah was her father's favourite, hadn't mattered for a long time.

Sarah smiled. 'We do. Oh doubtless, I'll meet a guy, and want to move on, but right now, for the time being…'

'Maybe Daddy will meet somebody.'

They looked at each other.

'I think it's a good idea,' Fran said. 'The moving in, I mean.'

At www.bridge.com there's a long list of webcams positioned on bridges throughout the world. Some are angled for the view: sunset on the Firth of Forth, sunrise over the Bay area from the Golden Gate. Others serve the same function as CCTV, security. Others monitor traffic flow.

Down in the basement Tony keeps his browser on www.bridge.com/lionsgate. He watches traffic; the flow of the cars over the narrow bridge is nearly continuous and, hence, soothing. There's no sound, but he can hear it anyway, the whoosh-whoosh like waves on the nearby beach. The bridge reminds him of Ireni, though he's not sure why. Sasha — there is that. But also, Vancouver itself; to Tony the bridge is emblematic of the city and thus, emblematic of his life, his marriage. Ireni. She's out there, somewhere, he thinks. Fran saw her. She's out there, isn't she?

But it's early morning and Tony is upstairs in the kitchen making himself breakfast when, downstairs, the monitor comes to life. There's a woman on the bridge, a woman walking slowly — the video streaming quality is poor, the connection slow, and on the screen the little figure's movements are jerky, stop-motion animated, as if a big hand rearranges her limbs between takes. And there she goes, up, climbing the railing. Up to the top, surprisingly athletic. She stands there, balanced, arms outstretched, and pauses for a moment, as though surveying the city, her domain.

And then she executes one last long beautiful swing out over the water, in the sunshine.

It will be two weeks before Ireni's body washes up; where could she have been during all that time, Tony will wonder, between jumping and, as it were, landing? He'll think, it's as though she's been on a cruise of the Pacific Northwest, but without a boat, and he'll smile, in spite of himself. She'll fetch up on Kitsilano Beach, the very beach she used to take her girls, the same beach where she found Sasha sleeping that time. It will take another two months before Ireni's body is identified, shortly after Tony files a missing person's report for the first time ever. He'd never thought of Ireni as missing before, just gone from him, sojourning. But he files the report and, sure enough, a few days later, he is asked to provide dental records. And then, one morning when he's working on his project in the basement, a policeman and woman will come to the door. They'll knock heavily and Tony will bound up the stairs and when he sees their faces, he'll know they've come about Ireni. And, after they've gone, he'll break down and cry, alone in his kitchen, alone in what he still thinks of as Ireni's house, the house he bought for his wife, his girls, and he'll cry like he has never cried all his adult life, his heart breaking for Ireni, his heart breaking all over again.

But none of this has happened yet, and Tony's in the kitchen, making himself a peanut butter and cheese sandwich.

And, at the same time, Fran is on yet another airplane; she's going home, back to London. Back to Nick. Back to Louis. She has a plan, she's going to take her life by the shoulders and give it a shake. Back to work — she has to, there is no choice. Things will be more, and less, like they used to be. Complicated.

How long have I been gone? Fran wonders. Eighteen days? Two and a half weeks? A lifetime?

She is wearing her linen dress, like the day she left London, and all she has with her now is her well-made leather handbag; she'll buy Nick some pink and white tulips when she lands. She gave the things Leslie bought her in Vegas to her mother that day, including the Caesars Palace t-shirt she'd been sleeping in. In her handbag she has a photo that Sarah gave her, of Tony and Sarah in the family room, and another of Leslie, standing on her own beneath a real estate 'For Sale' sign that bears her name. Tony has his arm around Sarah; Leslie is smiling broadly. Also in the handbag is a copy of the account of money Fran owes Leslie from Vegas, the extra fifty dollars added on at the bottom. But she isn't thinking about debts or photographs. She's thinking about Nick. And Louis.

ACKNOWLEDGMENTS

The author would like to thank Arts Council England for the Writer's Award of 2002 given toward the writing of this book, and the Royal Literary Fund, whose fellowship scheme has been of huge value. Thanks as well to Marilee Sigal, Lesley Bryce, and Rachel Calder for their close readings of early drafts; Peter and Ann Pullinger for the cabin at the lake; Carol Garton, Alixe Knighton, Julie Cruikshank, Garry Clarke, and Andrew Cullen for their advice on elements of the story, and Ellen Battle for Las Vegas.

Also by Kate Pullinger and published by Serpent's Tail

Where Does Kissing End?

Stephen Smith falls in love assuming that this is where happiness lies. The object of his desire is Mina Savage, the illegitimate child of parents themselves both illegitimate, a young woman whose ambitions and appetites outstrip Stephen's wildest fantasies. They become lovers. But when Mina continues to disappear at night, Stephen tries to force her to be faithful to him. Is Mina simply unfashionably promiscuous or is there something more sinister about her attitude toward other men?

Where Does Kissing End? is a novel about obsession and possession, a moral tale that asks where does pleasure end and where does the hurting begin?

'An extraordinary novel, intense, densely constructed; the sophisticated, highly-sexed and relentless pursuit of a chilling metaphor' *TLS*

'Aerating forbidden areas, tinged with porn, Kate Pullinger's short, bizarre fiction has a voice that will not be shouted down' *Mail on Sunday*

'An intriguing tale for those who like something a little unusual...superbly written, keeping you involved and guessing right to the end' *Cosmopolitan* (Australia)

'Precise, compelling... takes the metaphor of vampirism and explores its every crevice, to produce a very sexy depiction of *amour fou*' Leslie Dick

Also published by Serpent's Tail

We Need to Talk About Kevin, **winner of the Orange Prize for Fiction 2005**

'A book that acknowledges what many women worry about but never express: the fear of becoming a mother and the terror of what kind of child one might bring into the world' Jenni Murray

'An awesomely smart, stylish and pitiless achievement… Franz Kafka wrote that a book should be the ice-pick that breaks open the frozen seas inside us, because the books that make us happy we could have written ourselves. With *We Need to Talk About Kevin,* Shriver has wielded Kafka's axe with devastating force' *Independent*

'An elegant psychological and philosophical investigation of culpability with a brilliant denouement… although (Eva's) reliability as a narrator becomes increasingly questionable as she oscillates between anger, self-pity and regret, her search for answers becomes just as compulsive for the reader' *Observer*

'Harrowing, tense and thought-provoking, this is a vocal challenge to every accepted parenting manual you've ever read' *Daily Mail*

'One of the most striking works of fiction to be published this year. It is *Desperate Housewives* as written by Euripides… A powerful, gripping and original meditation on evil' *New Statesman*

Fiction
Non-fiction
Literary
Crime

Popular culture
Biography
Illustrated
Music

dare to read at serpentstail.com

Visit serpentstail.com today to browse and buy our books, and for exclusive previews, promotions, interviews with authors and forthcoming events.

NEWS — cut to the literary chase with all the latest news about our books and authors

EVENTS — advance information on forthcoming events, author readings, exhibitions and book festivals

EXTRACTS — read first chapters, short stories, bite-sized extracts

EXCLUSIVES — pre-publication offers, signed copies, discounted books, competitions

BROWSE AND BUY — browse our full catalogue, fill up a basket and proceed to our **fully secure** checkout - our website is your oyster

FREE POSTAGE & PACKING ON ALL ORDERS ANYWHERE!

---

sign up today and receive our new free full colour catalogue